The Miracle of the

Christmas Wish Holder

A novella

by R. A. Cabral

All Rights Reserved
Originally published in print
ISBN 978-0615552538
© 2011
www.phyllisscottpublishing.com

Edition 2
Republished by CreateSpace
ISBN: 978-1519195890
© 2015 R. A. Cabral

This book is a work of fiction. Names and characters, places and incidents are either products of the author's imagination or are used fictitiously. Any resemblance to actual events, locales or persons, living or dead, is entirely coincidental.

For the Audiobook dramatization of this work, please visit Audible.com, Amazon.com or iTunes.

ChristmasWishHolder.com

DEDICATION

This novel is dedicated to my late uncle,
Leroy Cardosa,
whose dream of a collaborative workshop
provided the genesis of this story.

The Miracle of the Christmas Wish Holder

CHAPTER ONE

The well-dressed woman in the gray pant suit arrived in front of the crimson brick building. She stopped to marvel at the craftsmanship of the all-brick entrance with its two turrets framing a circular brick faux window culminating at the apex. Soon she realized a man was standing inside the window display, attempting to balance on his front foot while tacking the right corner of a poster. She admired his tenacity. However, when the opposite corner came untacked, she watched with amusement as the left side of the three-foot-high banner came rolling toward him like a wave curling on the beach in Bolinas.

"Damn," the man laughed aloud. While gathering the banner, he remained unaware that anyone was watching from the sidewalk. A professional retail display specialist, this should have been the simplest of chores during this holiday season, yet it had turned into one of the most unpleasant. All of his San Francisco window displays had been completed weeks ago. He had returned to his hometown to assist his father and uncle in their annual holiday wooden toy creations. Jamas always came back in early December to decorate the storefront and the window display, with appropriate seasonal festoons, ribbons, and evergreen branches. But today required the sad chore of hanging this temporary paper sign that notified walk-in patrons that the Solteros had suspended sales of their famous Christmas Wish Holder, for what had become a Sacramento holiday tradition.

When Jamas finished tacking up the sign, he stood off to the side, reading it once more:

SOLTERO CHRISTMAS WISH HOLDERS
Temporarily "Off Sale"
Check Back Later This Week!

"Sad day." The woman's voice floated over the bell ringing inside the doorway.

Jamas turned and replied, "Sure is." He recognized the tall businesswoman, but couldn't recall her name. He remarked to himself that the color of her hair nearly matched the rich Rosewood wooden vessel sitting on the pedestal in the window.

She stuck out her right hand. "Grace McBride. You might remember me from high school, when my maiden name was. . . "

"Cech. . . Ceccarelli," Jamas interjected, "Donnie's girlfriend! I remember you." They exchanged smiles once more.

Grace nodded. "I'm here to see Ernie. Is he here?"

"Sure. C'mon in." Jamas led her inside the building, which served as a retail store and workshop combined. They passed the glass sales counter, where more of the ornately decorated Rosewood Christmas Wish Holders were stacked on shelves. Most of the space in this quaint brick building served as the brothers' workshop, with hand tools hanging on walls, inside wooden cubbies or scattered on tables. But the workshop was quiet now. Just a small pile of sawdust collected under the table where Rolando quietly sanded a child's toy. He looked up as his son escorted the woman toward the back.

"Uncle Ernie!" Jamas called. "You have a visitor."

Ernesto Soltero, the younger of the two retired brothers, emerged from the conference room. "Graciella!" he said, wrapping the woman in a friendly bear hug. "Como está?" His gray bearded whiskers tickled her neck. "Good to see you again, darlin'. C'mon in."

Ernie escorted her to a chair in front of the conference room table and walked around to the table's other side. "Gosh, you look great," he said. "It's been, what, at least five years since we bumped into each other at the mall that time?"

The woman laid her valise on the table and pulled out her Droid. "At least that long." She gestured toward the middle of the table where another of the Rosewood wooden boxes stood on top of a sheet of paper that contained the corporate logo of the Stoyonix Corporation. "This is your problem, I take it?"

"Yes, doggone it. One second, while I bring my brother in here," he said, holding out his left hand, while standing in the doorway. "Rollie!" he yelled, signaling with his right arm. "C'mon in here, will ya?"

Rolando Soltero, older and shorter than Ernesto, came in and sat down next to Grace. He wore an old fedora pulled low over his brow, which nearly disguised the gaze that remained fixed on the table. She noticed him casting a furtive glance out of the corner of his eye, which accentuated his gray mustache.

"Rollie, this is the PR gal, I was telling you about. . . Grace McBride. She owns Capital Communications." Grace shook hands with the mild-mannered brother.

"Alright, where to begin?" Ernie said, stroking his gray beard.

Pulling her sterling silver pen from the top of her writing pad, Graciella replied, "Always best to start at the beginning."

"Well, as I told you on the phone, we were hit with a threat of trademark infringement by that Stoyonix Corporation, up there in Nevada City. Infringement! Hell, I thought they were talking about that stuff that hung off of Buffalo Bill Cody's suede jacket."

Grace finished writing a sentence. "Trademark infringement is a serious matter. Have you thought about consulting an attorney?"

Rolando thumped the table. "My point exactly!"

"We haven't got time for that," Ernie countered. "By the time we got to court, I'll be planting tomatoes again, and none of the kids will get their Christmas Holders."

Grace asked him to start over, this time including how this year's version of the Holders attracted the attention of a $2 billion Internet company nestled in the Sierra Nevada foothills a little more than an hour's drive away.

For more than a decade, the retired construction workers Rolando and Ernesto Soltero had been making children's toys for sale at Christmas, first at Rollie's home, and then later in their 34th Street workshop. Cheap rent and close proximity to the downtown shopping district prompted them to lease this single-story brick building dating back to the last roar of the Roaring Twenties.

Over the past few years, their specialty evolved into making wooden Christmas "Wish Boxes," which were constructed out of rich pine and shaped like a cigar box. Enclosed in their "wish box" was a slip of paper instructing the child to write a wish for a grandparent or other relative and store it inside the box during the holidays. Then throughout the year they could use the wooden box to stash their favorite pencil, scissors and other trinkets. Moderately priced at $35, the handcrafted wish boxes sold out early in the season, and the Solteros donated the net profits to a local charity. The hand carved artwork, in combination with their philanthropic enterprise, engendered a loyal following in the Sacramento community.

Then this past summer, Ernesto's only child—Donte—had come up with the idea of creating a family logo to market their merchandise. A professional graphic designer, Donte had created logos for clients over the years, but this would be the first Soltero brand. As Donte's wife had passed away suddenly in late spring from pancreatic cancer, Ernesto encouraged his son in the development of the family logo, in part to help keep his mind off of the tragedy. It seemed to work, as he immersed himself in the project.

During the research phase, Donte delved into the lore of the Amazon rainforest, as their Portuguese heritage and family name originated in Brazil. Consequently, his design reflected the ethos of the Indian tribes. Moreover, he enhanced the mystique by securing a supply of Rosewood, a dark hardwood, which resulted in a richness and beauty never before reflected in the Soltero boxes.

Utilizing every inch of the expensive lumber, his design called for the container to be vertical instead of horizontal, and measure six inches in height, four inches in width by four inches in depth. The ultimate shape, size and beauty of this item called for something less utilitarian than a "box."

After more research, the family decided to call it a "wish holder," since it was shaped like a pencil holder from an office supply store. Once the children had made their holiday wishes, they could also use the object as a pen or pencil holder on their desk. Finally, Donte designed a custom printed card that would be attached by a string to the lid of the container. The instructions read:

Write Your Wish to Make Someone's Dream Come True
Drop this card inside. Close lid tight. And believe...

Enclosed with the batch of Rosewood lumber was a small doeskin packet that contained some of the original sawdust particles that resulted from the tree cuttings. Inside the pouch on a slip of paper was a brief warning written in Portuguese *salpique com moderação*. Translated it meant, "sprinkle sparingly." Recognizing the dust was intended to be incorporated in the final product, Donte sprinkled a minute amount over the top of each hand-painted, varnished logo. The act of sprinkling the dust upon the object ensured the wish would be granted through a spell supplied by the shaman of the tribe, he was told. As a lifelong Catholic, Donte had witnessed priests sprinkling holy water and incense as a means of blessing an object. Surely, this shamanic ritual couldn't be much different. For the final step, something he came up with through experimentation, he "baked" the holders in his oven at home to seal in the decorative properties, just as he had watched Uncle Richie do with his Raku pottery pieces many years ago in Oregon. The ultimate effect made the image jump to life.

Last year, Solteros sold more than 250 of the pinewood Christmas boxes. This year, to help cover the cost of the more expensive Rosewood, and because demand last season far exceeded supply, they increased their output to 500 units. Meantime, expenses had risen nearly threefold, so it was critical that they sold each box—*holder*—produced.

Their problems began when the wife of State Senator Dawson purchased one of the first Rosewood variety Christmas Wish Holders for her youngest child, and displayed the unique object at a Christmas party the senator hosted in mid-December. In attendance that day was Stoyonix Company CEO, Ronko Stoyonovich, who viewed the object and immediately thought he saw a similarity in the Soltero logo to his company's corporate logo. In short order, his legal team dispatched a "cease and desist" letter, warning the Solteros of the company's intention to file a trademark infringement suit in state court should the Solteros continue selling the wooden collectible this holiday season.

Since it was known Donte was still grieving over the death of his wife, Rollie didn't want to castigate his nephew over the problem. For that reason he reluctantly agreed to at least meet with this high level PR woman that came highly recommended by his brother.

The sound of the Droid vibrating on the table interrupted Ernie's presentation. Grace snapped up the personal device and read a quick text message. "Excuse me one second? The office needs me to confirm something—the mayor's office is calling about an event tonight." She sent off a reply and placed the device back inside her coat jacket.

Ernie said, "Well, that's where we are: stuck here with 500 Christmas boxes, that we dare not sell or otherwise incur the wrath of Stoyonovich, who's worth several billion dollars, and can delay this thing until doomsday."

"Not to mention ruin us financially," added Rollie.

Jamas, who had been leaning against the doorjamb with his arms folded, listening to the conversation, chimed in. "My dad can't afford any legal bills, not on top of my mom's current medical condition," said the slender man. "We need to be prudent in our decision here." The profundity of his statement quieted the group. "I'm just sayin'."

"No, no, we understand you're just watchin' after your folks, Jimmy," Ernest said. "But again, we can't make 500 new boxes in time for Christmas. Hell, we got people driving by looking in the window waiting for the sale sign to go live. It's a little more than one week before Christmas. If we go the legal route, we're done for this season."

After listening intently, it appeared to Grace they had only one solution: Donate the objects to a local charity and take the tax write-off. "If I may recommend one, perhaps the Saint Celestin Orphanage." She offered that she might come up with something more productive after consulting with her staff, but given the extreme deadline and restrictive circumstances, this seemed like the logical choice. "If you like, I can arrange a meeting with the Stoyonix legal team, maybe as early as tomorrow," she offered. Reluctantly, the Solteros all agreed. Grace promised to prepare a one-page written summary of the action points for their review by end of the day.

Escorting her toward the door, Ernie thanked Graciella for coming and told her to include an estimate for her time. The woman shook her head and smiled. "I'm doing this 'pro bono.' It's the least I can do, given the holiday season, and your situation."

Outside the doorway, she turned and asked, "How's Donte these days?"

The older man folded his arms across his powder blue denim shirt, pursed his lips and nodded. "Well, you may have heard he's still getting over the loss of his wife. It's been hard on him, you know. All in all, he's doing. . . not too bad."

She nodded. "And the kids, how are they taking it?"

"Aw, they're great. Alena's in her first year at Sonoma State and Anthony's a junior in high school. In fact, Alena's home now on vacation, helpin' her dad around the house."

She nodded again, self-consciously. "I was hoping he would be here today. Haven't seen him in a really long time."

Ernie explained that Donte, in fact, was meeting with a vendor friend that morning, exhausting every avenue possible for modifying the Holders in the hope of avoiding the potential injunction. One experiment they recently tried called for the physical removal of the logo, but Donte had used a high-tech pressure beading process for applying the color and the excision made for a sloppy and scarred face. They even considered taking apart the five-sided objects and replacing the front face, but the joints had been secured with a strong epoxy and would not come apart without damaging the wood.

"I'm sure you'll catch up with him before this is all through."

"Good to hear," Graciella responded, walking around to the driver's side of her Jaguar. "Great to see you, Ernesto. I'll get started on this as soon as I get back to the office."

* * *

That evening, Donte stood in the kitchen of his Pocket Area home intently watching the highlights of a college basketball game while braising chicken on the Jenn-Aire stovetop. Still rail lean from years of racquetball, he retained a youthful-looking physique for forty five, and if not for the nearly gray head of hair, could even pass for late thirties. Anthony, his sixteen-year-old son was sitting on the couch, watching it along with him on the wall screen, while Alena was setting the table.

"When's the last time you saw a game, Dad?" she asked. "In person." Donte's facial expression told her it had been so long he couldn't recall. "You really need to get out more. Have some fun. I'm worried about you," she said, patting the back of his shirt.

"Don't worry about me, dear," Donte said, taking a swig from his beer bottle.

Anthony looked up from the couch with a disdainful expression. "I was talking to dad," she said in her brattiest sister voice. Anthony smiled and turned back to the television. It was so good to have Alena back home again, especially during the holidays.

Taking up her case again, she noted "You really need to get out, I mean like out partying." Her father's scowl prompted her to add, "I'm just sayin'."

The wall phone rang. Alena answered. "Soon. . . I promise. I'm still unpacking. When are you going to come over for dinner? How 'bout tonight? No? Okay. Here's dad," she said handing the yellow phone to her father. "Grandpa."

Ernie mentioned that Graciella McBride came by that afternoon, met with them, and had some good ideas for getting them out of the jam. Donte thought they were going to wait until he came back with his final report. Ernie next asked how it went with the vendor Donte visited earlier in the day. "No dice, Dad. We're stuck. Made these things too damn well, apparently." Alena glanced over to see a rare chuckle from her father. "Tonight? I suppose. Yeah, sure, meet you there."

After dinner, Donte slipped on his jacket and told Alena he was going out for a while. She brightened at the thought her father was taking her advice, but when she learned he was just going out to meet her grandfather at the tavern, she simply shrugged.

CHAPTER TWO

When Donte pushed the plush Naugahyde cinnabar red doors and entered Jericho's Tavern the smell of bourbon and cheap perfume attacked his olfactory sense. And it felt wonderful. He realized his daughter was right; it had been too long since he had been out for a simple nightcap or a Sunday beer. For a Tuesday evening, the crowd was spirited and most of the bar stools were occupied. He walked behind the patrons, searching for the broad backside of Ernesto Soltero, who by this time should have been regaling some poor soul with one of his famous fishing stories.

The bartender looked up to take Donte's order. "Sammy. . . my pop here?"

"Haven't seen him, Donnie. What can I get ya?"

"Sierra on tap?" Donte gestured to the beer spigots.

"You got it." The barman nodded, turned and filled a glass.

Since he couldn't find two empty bar stools, he took the nearest available booth facing the door. Donte slipped off his jacket and waited. Looking around the room he saw sporadic signs of holiday decoration. Sam had a good heart, he thought.

When the doors opened, in walked a stunningly beautiful tall brunette, immediately catching Donte's eye. Her hair had been piled up high with tresses adorning her cheeks in the fashion of a Greek goddess. She certainly looked out of place here at the Tavern. When she waved and approached, Donte was floored. He slipped out of the booth and reached out to give Graciella McBride, his former high school sweetheart, a polite hug. The perfume, matched the image; it was intoxicating.

"Great to see you!" she said, pulling off the black winter coat, revealing a forest green blouse with three inches of cleavage. Recognizing the look on his face, she added, "I just came from a reception for the opening of the new Railyards project. I served on the mayor's original task force. I didn't know you were coming, too. Is your father here?"

"Apparently, he's. . . late." Donte noticed that several of the bar stool patrons were still staring in her direction. Up close, he saw that her hair had been injected with feint blonde streaks to hide the first signs of gray.

"Really, good to see you," she said again. "Been at least ten years, I think." She opened her valise and gestured to a paper inside. "Anyway. . . in the short time I've had, I came up with a few ideas I think will help save the Soltero family tradition from a legal battle." Graciella's smile did more to light up the booth than any candle holder ever could.

He offered to buy her a drink and she nodded politely. Waiting for Sam to mix her Grey Goose martini, Donte found his fingers nervously tapping the wooden rail. When he turned with the martini, she was watching him walk back to the table. He carefully placed the glass stem on the table, and slid the drink over to her, ensuring it didn't spill.

She offered proper consolation for the death of his wife and asked how the two children were doing, even though Ernie had provided an update earlier that day. By the time she had finished tactfully eliciting personal information, Grace was fully briefed on the highlights of Donte's past ten years, a tactic she had mastered in becoming one of Sacramento's elite public relations pros.

Donte looked at his watch. "I don't know what could be keeping him."

"Is he normally this late?"

"Almost never. I'm gonna call him." Donte started to reach for his jacket pocket, but before he bent down Grace's Droid was staring him in the face, casting a red glow. He could hear it ringing and saw the readout: "Ernie S". He picked up the device.

"Dad, it's me. Say, where are you?" After a pause, he added "Yeah, she's here. . . Okay. Alright." Donte studied the Droid to find the "end" button, but Graciella grabbed it and adroitly concluded the call in one quick motion. "Well, apparently, he's not feeling well now. I dunno." Donte appeared embarrassed. "And he said we should go ahead with the meeting, as I'm fully capable of handling 'the family business.'" He made the quote gesture with his fingers.

She recognized his sigh of relief and weighed the mixed emotions. "Were you worried about him?"

"Yeah, I was afraid he may have been in an accident, even though it's less than ten blocks away. He's getting on, ya know." Donte gestured toward the paper on her valise. "Let's see what you got there."

What Grace had come up with was a glorified version of her original solution: Soltero family would agree to change its marketing brand, in exchange for the right to donate the Christmas Wish Holders to a local charity, in this case the Saint Celestin Orphanage, on whose board of directors she served as a regent.

"Your father and uncle were amenable to this idea, earlier. So, if you agree, I'll call to set up a meeting where we can present this in person to the Stoyonix legal department."

Donte scratched his mustache. "Yeah, but this doesn't address the financial contribution we always make to the local charity. Since we can't sell the Holders, there's no income, and we certainly can't make a financial donation without the proceeds."

"How much were you counting on this year?" She sipped from the martini glass.

"At least ten grand. We were selling them for $50 each. We made 500 and more than half of the take would offset our production costs, rent and other operational expenses. Most of that is on my credit card," he smiled wryly. "We figured we'd clear about ten."

"Look, Donte. Your first priority should be to get this legal gorilla off your back. And the only way to do that is to address their position that you won't infringe on their trademark. I think *this*," she snapped the paper with her middle finger "will placate them." The look on her face indicated there wasn't much else to discuss. "I'll call first thing in the morning and see if we can set a meeting for later in the day. You coming?"

"Yeah, I guess I'm representin' the family in this

case."

"Alright then." She closed the valise, and started to slide out of the Naugahyde booth.

"Okay, but meantime, I've still got one other idea for modifying the Holder."

While slipping into her coat, she smiled. Although adorable, her former boyfriend was naïve still. As they walked out of the bar, Donte waved to the bartender and walked Grace to her car.

* * *

Around eleven the next morning Ernesto arrived at the workshop and found his son standing in front of the door, hands in his pockets, bouncing from one foot to the next trying to keep warm. Temperatures were in the low thirties, a bit colder than average for Sacramento in December. Forecasters reported that it might snow later in the week near the 1,000 foot elevation.

"Why aren't you inside?" Ernie shouted above the clatter of the garbage truck, scooping up cans over on the next street.

"Aw, I forgot my key, and I'm waiting for Graciella. She's picking me up and we're driving up to Stoyonix for a meeting. I thought you'd be here by now."

"Good, good," Ernie said, rubbing his hands for warmth before slipping the key in the door lock.

"So, you, uh, feeling better?" he asked, following his father inside the workshop.

Ernie turned up the thermostat along the wall.

"What?"

"Last night. . . said you weren't feelin' up to par."

Ernie waved off his son. "Eh."

Donte picked up the prototype they'd left on the counter after yesterday's meeting, and covered it with an elegant colorful scarf. "I'm thinkin'. . . it was a set up."

His father waved him off once again. "And what if it was. Enjoy the ride. Nothin' like female companionship, son."

Donte shrugged. "It's too soon for that," he said. "Maria's been gone nearly. . . " He struggled in his estimation, so much time had passed.

"Six months," the father assisted him. "It's never too soon to get back up on the horse, son. I'm just sayin'."

"You never 'got back on the horse'."

"Because when your mom passed, I was already an old geezer. But you, you're still young. You've got vitality! Lots of life left to live."

"I've got the kids, that's enough vitality." Donte looked out the main window, checking for his ride.

"That's not what I mean, and you know it," Ernie chided his son. "Tell me you think she's not a hot dish."

"Who?"

"Who? Who're we talking about—Graciella, for criminy sakes!"

"She's. . ."

"What? She looks hot to me, and I'm a geezer. You tellin' me you don't find her attractive?"

"She's alright—for a gal in her mid-40s. Now, will you get off it?" He stuck his hands back inside his jacket and looked out the window at the Libby, McNeill & Libby Cannery complex. He stared admiringly at the old red brick building constructed around 1915 and recently refurbished into office spaces. "Besides, she's outta my league."

Just then, they heard two beeps from Grace's Jaguar, which had pulled up to the curb.

Ernie patted his son on the back. "Go get 'em, son. And bring back some good news."

* * *

Traveling east on Interstate 80, Donte enjoyed the comforts of the Jaguar's interior. In the roomy, comfortable leather seats, he held the Christmas Wish Holder prototype in his lap like a prized possession. It was wrapped in a beautiful scarf with florid rainforest designs. He peeled away the scarf and exposed the rich, dark wooden object. When the sunlight streaked through the window, it created an enchanting warm glow inside the vehicle.

"Please, tell me that didn't come from the Amazon rainforest," Grace said. From behind her dark glasses, he couldn't tell if she was teasing or serious.

"Well. . . it's Bolivian Rosewood."

She smiled. "Yeah—same difference."

"Seriously. I purchased the wood through a contact who works with the local Indians down there. He swore to me, the tribe sanctioned the sale of this timber. In fact, it's from second-stand growth. And to sweeten the deal, he tossed in a bag of magick dust that came from the wood cuttings and was blessed by the shaman of that tribe."

Grace appeared less than impressed.

As the road began to climb, gaining elevation, they passed lush forests of evergreen and pine trees that engulf this region of the foothills. In places there was a smattering of snow on the ground.

Donte fingered the "S" design of the Holder, tracing its elegant and fluid line through sweeping curves with his index finger. Watching from the corner of her eye, Grace's heart began to race, as she fantasized a lover's touch, caressing and sensitive. The complete opposite of her former husband, the commercial real estate salesman.

"This whole logo design, rainforest Rosewood. . . really means something to you, doesn't it?"

Donte thought to formulate his response before speaking. Her question appeared sincere, yet it suspiciously sounded like the disbelieving heart of one who has never been touched by magick. By "magick" he meant the term normally associated with the paranormal application, that is "any willed action leading to intended change," not conventional stage magic. He found himself believing in it ever more since delving into the mystical shamanistic world of healing and astral projection. He now believed in *possibilities*. And he also remembered that Grace had led a more grounded existence and would not easily accept "flights of fancy," certainly not without evidence. And at this juncture of his life, he had little evidence with which to prove this new concept. But as Donte continued to navigate through the emotional loss that death had delivered to him, it had opened his heart to becoming more trusting and vulnerable. In the spirit of trust, in this rekindled relationship, he elected to share his belief with her.

"Yes, this simple design matters to me because it symbolizes things that are natural and good. It originates from a place of beauty and resonates with the spirit of the woodlands. And I hope, in some small way, I've turned it into something meaningful for my family; something that'll last and maybe become a tradition. I think it may have the potential to change lives."

"You mean, through the granting of the wishes?"

He nodded. She appeared to be warming up to the idea; at least not rejecting it immediately.

Graciella smiled once more, secure in the gentleness and sincerity of this man, whom she had known before turning thirteen. She realized now that his sensitive qualities had been obscured when they were entwined as loving teenagers.

They transitioned from Interstate 80 onto Highway 49, a two-lane road that plowed through the scenic beauty of Placer County. Snow was now piled several feet high in places. One home had decorated its evergreen tree with oversized Christmas bells and lights hanging from the branches.

Soon, they were traveling through the old mining city of Grass Valley. Minutes later they arrived at their destination: the Stoyonix corporate campus, secluded from the bustling freeway traffic in the cloistered beauty of the Nevada City pine trees in a winter wonderland.

CHAPTER THREE

While they snapped on their security badges in the lobby, a red-headed legal assistant named Barnswell had come to escort them to the Legal Department conference room. As they walked through the hallways, Donte noticed that everything about Stoyonix was gleaming, metallic, and shining, a stark contrast to the rustic pine groves that shielded their headquarters.

Donte and Grace settled in the black leather swivel chairs around an onyx table across from Barnswell and a petite blonde in her mid-twenties, Ms. Cox. They informed Grace that the company's Legal Counsel would not be joining them this afternoon, as he had been called away due to a family medical matter. As Grace had requested the meeting, she opened her valise and took out copies of her one-page presentation, a brief summary of the Soltero's offer.

She slid two of the copies across the table just when the conference room door opened. In walked a middle-aged, well-dressed man who acted as if he owned the place. Ronko Stoyonovich entered and quickly told his legal assistants not to get up, that he just came in to say hello to their guests, and. . . Ronko paused mid-sentence. "You look very familiar," he said to Grace, brushing his thick shock of black hair from his forehead. "Didn't I see you the other night at Senator Dawson's. . . ?"

". . . Grace McBride." The woman stood quickly, interrupting with her right hand outstretched. "And this is Donte Soltero," she said, gesturing behind her. She succeeded in shifting attention away from the CEO's allusion to the Dawson party, where she had personally witnessed the Stoyonovich explosion over the Wish Holder. It was a fairly intimate party, where the guests numbered fewer than 75, and nearly everyone witnessed or heard the outburst. Graciella had a ringside view, as she had just replaced the object on the mantle, explaining to Senator Dawson that she knew the family who had produced the unique holiday gift item, when Stoyonovich picked it up and began complaining loudly that the design was an obvious rip-off of the Stoyonix corporate logo. After several minutes, Dawson diffused the situation by having the mayor escort Stoyonovich outside to the heated patio area, but not before Ronko snapped a picture of the object with his smartphone and left the living room. At Senator Dawson's request, Grace provided a contact at the Solteros workshop, suggesting he speak with Ernesto. He asked if he could mention her name, and she volunteered her services, should the Solteros see the need. A few days later, she took the call from Ernesto Soltero asking for the meeting. Grace intentionally withheld the fact that, in effect, she had self-referred her firm's services. Here in the Stoyonix conference room, she saw no value in revealing that information either to Donte or Ronko Stoyonovich.

The CEO stared at her quizzically. "Assume you are their attorney?"

"Uh, no," Grace said. "But I am representing the Soltero family. I own a public relations firm—Capital Communications."

"Yes, of course. Well, I didn't mean to interrupt. I'm sure they told you that Mr. Rigl unfortunately had to miss this meeting, as his daughter is undergoing cancer treatments. In fact, he's down there in Sacramento right now with her."

"Sorry to hear that," Grace replied.

"But you're in good hands here. And this matter shouldn't be too difficult to resolve, really. We understand these things happen," he said, cleaning the outer edge of his ear with his index finger, "a small mom and pop hires out their logo design to one of these fly-by-night Internet companies, and without knowing it, you've just bought a corporate logo rip-off without. . . "

"Excuse me," Donte interrupted, "but we didn't pay anyone for our logo design. . . "

Ronko's smile revealed a small gap between the front teeth. "My point exactly."

"No, sir, I created this logo myself. I'm a professional designer, and I spent a fair amount of time researching this design." Ronko's continual smile attempted to hide the fierce animosity brewing inside. "And I can assure you that I did not model my design after your firm's logo. In fact, to my eye, it's not even. . . "

"Perhaps . . . not intentionally," Stoyonovich interrupted and subtly tipped his head to the side to communicate that the conversation had just concluded.

Grace broke the silence. "Mr. Stoyonovich, after we share our proposal with your people here, I'm sure we'll come to a mutually beneficial solution."

"I'm sure you will," he said curtly, nodding to his legal assistants as he left the conference room. "Please continue."

Grace took a breath to allow the air to clear and to center her focus. She began by stating that although Soltero brothers were not admitting infringement of the Stoyonix trademark, in the spirit of the season (and to avoid an expensive court case) they would agree to cease and desist immediately from merchandising the image on future products. The Christmas Wish Holders, she informed them, could have generated an estimated $25,000.

She placed the prototype Christmas Wish Holder on the conference room table. The blonde attorney reached over and raised the object to her eyes. She studiously examined the logo, comparing the signature marks of this design to the page she was holding of her company's corporate logo. She passed the object to Barnswell, who glanced at it with less interest.

Grace covered the Soltero's proposal point by point:

- Soltero brothers, an unincorporated enterprise, agree not to sell the holiday holders, thereby technically eliminating any potential infringement of Stoyonix. With Stoyonix permission, Solteros will donate the Holders to a local Sacramento orphanage;

- In future, Solteros agree to redesign the logo to not infringe on Stoyonix trademark;

- In return, to compensate the charity, Solteros request that Stoyonix donate $5,000 to a charity of the family's choice, since Solteros had expected to generate at least twice this amount in net revenue through the sale of their holiday Holders.

The Stoyonix attorneys sat across the table, flabbergasted. Ms. Cox knew they held all the cards and

McBride was attempting to play on their goodwill by issuing an audacious request. She visually checked with Barnswell, who as the junior attorney nodded for her to assume the leadership role. Cox, who attempted to emulate the confidence of her CEO, but generated only the arrogance, stated:

"Miss McBride. . . Mr. Soltero. . . here is Stoyonix' counter-proposal:

- Solteros may donate the Holders to the orphanage, so long as they agree to remove the image from the Holder, and inscribe on the 'scrubbed face' the words *Christmas Wish Holders donated courtesy of Stoyonix Corporation*;

- Secondly, Solteros agree to change its logo for future;

- Stoyonix will pay no monetary damages for loss of revenue these actions may cause the Soltero family operation."

Donte stood up forcefully, his leather chair sliding three feet behind him. "I'll meet you in the car," he said to Grace.

* * *

Donte dropped his badge at the security station and walked out of Stoyonix' stainless steel and glass building. Slushing through the parking lot, he wondered whether the Rosewood might not have been original stand rainforest timber, complete with its very own curse. Otherwise, how else to explain this run of bad luck?

When the offer to purchase the wood had come in from his distant cousin Martin, he was assured everything had been above board. Martin worked in importing/exporting in his home city of Belém do Pará, Brazil. He claimed he had an excellent source for the Bolivian Rosewood, which had been cultivated on plantation lands, not harvested from original stands of rainforest timber. Donte took small comfort in knowing the name Belém translated from the Portuguese means Bethlehem, the home of Jesus Christ.

Over the years Donte had become environmentally enlightened and more aware of the sensitivities surrounding Amazonian rainforests, where deforestation has occurred at an eye popping 35-percent annual rate since the 1990s. For that reason, he hoped that Martin hadn't been tricked into taking pristine rainforest timber for the Holders.

* * *

Graciella exited the Stoyonix building and glared at Donte the entire time it took her to walk toward the vehicle. She remotely popped open the car's doors and got in without speaking. After starting the engine, Grace removed her sunglasses. "You want to tell me what that was all about?"

Donte rubbed his cold hands together. "I was hoping you were going to enlighten me."

"What is that supposed to mean?" she tossed her valise in the back seat, drove out of the parking lot and headed for the highway. They traveled briskly along the inlet road. "I'm still waiting," Grace said.

"You know, when Stoyonovich entered the room, he

mentioned having seen you last week. Would that happen to have been at Senator Dawson's party?"

Grace calmly steered the vehicle onto Highway 49, glancing casually behind her in the rear view mirror, as sheets of icy white powder streamed behind the vehicle.

"Yes, you couldn't help but notice him that night, he made such a commotion about your Wish Holder. Dawson had someone take him outside to calm him down."

Donte nodded. "And whose idea was it to have Dawson call my father, warning him of the possible litigation by Stoyonix?"

"The senator's," she said. "Look. We go way back. I didn't want to see your family slammed by an injunction. Besides, time was of the essence."

Donte appeared satisfied with her explanation. He wondered why it hadn't come out the previous evening.

"So, what did you hope to accomplish by storming out of the meeting?" she asked. "It certainly wasn't very professional."

"Look, we've already tried removing the logo from one of the prototypes," Donte explained. "Didn't work. Completely ruined the face of the box. So, that's not an option. Besides, we put nearly 300 man hours into hand carving and decorating those images."

She glanced over at him. "You're kidding."

"No! Each of those logos was hand carved, using a burnishing tool to remove the excess wood, leaving only the raised edge of the logo."

She drove quietly, with a deeper appreciation for the skill required of the project.

"I didn't realize that."

"Only Uncle Rollie could do that job. There's nobody who could touch that kind of painstaking craftsmanship, standing hunched over a table for hours, carefully carving and burnishing the wood like that. It's a lost art." He noticed she appeared calmer now. "Not to mention, the hours it took me to hand paint the logo, decorate the flourishes and embellishments. That's Old World craftsmanship. Not the digitized version of reality they specialize in."

Donte sighed and rubbed his face. "Aw, who am I kidding? Should have never got us into this fix to begin with."

She reached over and patted his knee. "Don't be too hard on yourself. We'll think of something." She already was formulating a response to the Stoyonix counter offensive.

* * *

Had she followed the Internet/computer software industry more closely, Grace McBride would have been aware that MacroVision Corporation had dangled a potential merger/buyout proposition to Stoyonix company executives earlier that fall, and that CEO Stoyonovich wanted nothing to interfere with his secret negotiations. Consequently, Stoyonovich was trying stridently to avert negative publicity and wanted to dispense with this trademark infringement issue quietly.

Ronko Stoyonovich was the quintessential American dreamer. Born in Czechoslovakia in 1968, the year the Soviet empire asserted a strong fist over the country, he grew up an aggressive, intellectual child of a Russian soldier and Czech mother. Eventually, he attended university at Bratislava and participated in the anti-Communist student rallies there in fall 1989. Soon after that crackdown, he escaped and relocated to the United States on a student visa. He completed his science degree at UCLA. Following graduation he gained U.S. citizenship and moved to Silicon Valley where he worked for Hewlett-Packard and SynchTronics.

Realizing he needed an advanced degree to attain his goals of someday owning and operating a successful Silicon Valley startup, in 1996 Stoyonovich attended Stanford where he pursued a master's in computer science. There he met fellow graduate students Larry Page and Sergey Brin, who were working on a new web browser they initially called BackRub. By February 1999, when he joined their new company, the owners had changed the company's name to Google.

Ronko Stoyonovich contributed to Google's early success and stayed on through the glory years when they became the world's leader in web search. About the time Google went public, and enriched its employees beyond imagination, Stoyonovich had fallen into disfavor with management. He quietly resigned his position, some said over the possibility of *i-spionage*. He left wealthy, but under a cloud of suspicion.

Consequently, the last thing he needed with the MacroVision merger pending was a new round of negative publicity to reopen the old rumors he had worked tirelessly to bury.

* * *

Later that afternoon, Ms. Cox entered the office of the Legal Counsel. She placed a copy of the memo summarizing their meeting with the Solteros in the in-basket. Then she laid the Soltero Christmas Wish Holder on the corner of Rigl's desk, next to the stacks of mail and correspondence that had been piling up, ever since his daughter had taken a downward turn in her bout with pancreatic cancer.

* * *

After dinner that evening, Alena found Donte working in his home studio. On the desk was an exploded hard copy printout of the Stoyonix logo. On the computer screen, she could see the same logo embedded in a line of words.

"Dad, isn't that how you got into trouble in the first place?"

Donte looked up at his daughter's face. She was the only one alive who could pound him so bluntly, but he knew she was only motivated by her concern. And he loved her for it.

"Actually, I'm working on a new solution to fix the problem."

"Huh? Aren't you just blatantly copying that company's logo right now?"

"Sweetheart, I am attempting to create the artwork for the backside of the card on the Wish Holder, to give Stoyonix what they want: corporate sponsorship."

"But they didn't make the Holders; you and grandpa and great Uncle Rollie made them. Why give them any credit in the first place?"

"Because, apparently, I made our Soltero logo too close to the Stoyonix logo, and we're going to ask them to be like 'partners' in the project. So they don't sue us back to the stone age." Her father's boyish smile told her that everything might be alright again.

"Cool," she said, quietly closing the studio door behind her.

* * *

That evening, long after the cleaning crew had finished, Legal Counsel Bernard Rigl entered the Stoyonix building, climbed the stairs and walked into his expansive office. Foregoing the bright overhead lights, he walked toward his leather swivel chair and turned on the desk lamp. He sat down, examined the two huge stacks of mail on the desk, and the discouraging pile of correspondence in his in-basket, and collapsed in his chair. He buried his face in his large, smooth hands and quietly began to sob.

A plump, balding man in his late fifties, Rigl was an original member of the Stoyonix executive team. With a mid-level, six-figure income and stock options worth millions, he was set for life. But for the past three weeks he had been living a life of torment, driving daily down to the UC Davis Medical Center in Sacramento, where his daughter was fighting for her life. It was agonizing to see her being bombarded with new experimental treatments each week. The hospital's oncology specialists had tried every new approach known in the western hemisphere. The only thing they hadn't attempted was the services of a local witch doctor.

He looked up and across the darkened room. Apparently, someone (one of his staff, no doubt) had fastened a holiday wreath to his office door, obviously to foster "Christmas cheer" in this bleak period of his life. As his wife had been gone for nearly a decade, he had believed he was impervious to sadness. But, clearly, he was unprepared for another fatal illness, especially in his last living family member. Especially at Christmas.

Rigl shook himself and prepared to dive into the correspondence first, as documents requiring his signature would have top priority and he wasn't sure how much stamina he had left this evening. As he reached for the in-basket, he nearly knocked over the wooden Christmas Wish Holder that sat on the corner of his desk. He brought it under the lamp for closer inspection. Instantly, he recognized the logo as that of the trademark infringer. But he'd only been shown a camera picture view. Up close, he marveled at the detailed, exquisite craftsmanship in the carving of the face of the object. He also saw for the first time that this design was only similar to the Stoyonix corporate logo, not the slam dunk, cheap imitation he was first led to believe from the image in the distorted, pixilated picture "Stoyo" had shoved at him in a rage.

The card that was attached to the lid by a simple white string caught his attention. He flipped over the card and read the instructions:

*Write Your Wish to Make
Someone's Dream Come True*
Drop this card inside. Close lid tight. And believe . . .

Believe, he thought. And while his mind clung gingerly to that simple concept, his eyes wandered back to the wreath on the door. It reminded him of happier times as a boy, growing up in Michigan, when Christmas time meant the renewed belief in the spirit of Saint Nicholas, and the promise of the little Christ child.

He removed the white card from the lid of the Rosewood Wish Holder and laid it on his desk. He slipped the Mont Blanc writing pen from the inside jacket pocket, paused momentarily and then wrote the words: **Kimmie—Cancer Free**. He placed the card inside the Holder and closed the lid tightly. And *believed*.

CHAPTER FOUR

Early next morning, Donte phoned Capital Communications from his kitchen table. Grace hadn't arrived in the office yet, so he left a "quasi-urgent" message for her to call back. He thought to try her cell, but didn't feel comfortable yet with that move. Besides, she hadn't invited him to use her direct mode of communication. This way, it was more... *professional.*

Alena shuffled into the kitchen, eyes squinting from the light overhead, her hair a tousled mess. She'd been out late the night before with former classmates from high school. "Morning," she said, yawning and pulling a coffee mug down from the cupboard.

"Well, look who the cat dragged in."

She poured a cup of coffee and sat down at the kitchen table, opposite Donte. She grabbed for the features section of the paper and noticed her father nervously tapping the table, staring down at the floor. "What's up?"

Donte looked up, surprised. "Nothin'." Alena's frowny yet sleepy facial expression suggested she wasn't having any of it. Donte knew better than to expect morning patience from Alena. "I'm not sure what to do."

"About?" she said, yawning again, with the coffee mug poised next to her mouth.

"My next move. On this logo-lawsuit thing. Not sure

whether to call grandpa now or wait until I hear back from this PR gal. I just left a message for her."

Alena slurped from the cup. "That the one you were all hot for in high school?" Donte returned the frowny facial expression, prompting his daughter to giggle.

"Say, when are we going to decorate that poor Christmas tree over there?" she asked. "It's been sitting in the corner all barren since I got home."

"Got any plans this morning?" he asked, grabbing for the phone. Alena's eyes widened as she shook her head. "We'll do it after breakfast, then."

He punched in a number and held the phone to his ear. Ernest picked up on the second ring. "Hey, Dad. I wanted to update you on our meeting yesterday." His father asked if he planned to come over to the workshop. "Not until this afternoon. We're decorating the tree this morning." He smiled at Alena. "I know, Dad, 'time's a'wastin.' That's why I'm calling."

Donte summarized the meeting at Stoyonix, hitting the high points, but omitting his standoff with the company CEO. He and Graciella were both working on parts of their counter-proposal to the Stoyonix attorneys, and should know something more by end of the day.

Ernest groused, "Well, we're losin' daylight."

"I know, Dad." Donte had heard the old farmer's expression his whole life, one of the vestiges from Grandpa Antonio, who once farmed the Pocket Area along the Sacramento River in south Sacramento. "I'll hook up with you later over at the workshop."

* * *

Donte went up into the attic and pulled down the boxes of Christmas decorations. Alena helped by lowering the cartons to the garage floor. They spent most of the morning decorating the tree, drinking coffee and listening to Christmas music on the radio. Each time the news interrupted at the top of the hour, he thought about calling Graciella again, but held off. Finally, he figured he'd give her until lunch time.

A few minutes before noon, Anthony trudged into the kitchen, ignoring his family in the living room. Without even a grumbled "good morning," he grabbed a box of cereal and a bowl and laid them on the table. As he reached into the refrigerator, Alena yelled across the room, "Forget cereal; it's almost time for lunch."

"Whatever," Anthony replied sleepily, plopping down at the table.

The phone rang. Anthony stared at the handset, and read the name on the Caller ID. "Dad. Someone at the Capitol." Donte handed the string of lights to his daughter and headed into the kitchen. Anthony tossed the phone underhanded to him, like a pitcher softly throwing to first base after fielding a bunt.

It was Grace. She'd been busy with meetings all morning, and this was her first opportunity to return his call. Another reason for the delay, she explained, was that she was waiting for a return call from Stoyonix.

"Really?" Donte was curious.

"Yep, this morning, I placed a call to the company's vice president of corporate communications. She hasn't called back yet. In fact, after we get off here, I am going to send her an email."

His curiosity was piqued. "And, it will say. . . "

Grace pulled up the email and read it verbatim. "Subject line: Grinch Time. Subhead: "Baby, It's Coal Outside" (she spelled the word 'coal' so he would get the pun over the phone).

"On behalf of the Soltero family, and their famous Christmas Wish Holders, we wish you 'Happy Holidays.' And strongly suggest that you emulate the Three Wise Men, and counsel your legal department to reconsider our written offer, which proffered a reasonable solution to this ridiculous trademark infringement matter.

"If we do not hear back from you by noon tomorrow, affirming our proposal, we will be advising news media throughout Northern California, the Associated Press, CNN and all those bloggers who love to hurl virtual snowballs that if they are searching for a heartfelt weekend story we will gladly share an updated version of 'The Grinch Who Stole Christmas,' about an Internet giant who is ruining the holidays for a group of Sacramento orphans.

"For good measure, we will be forwarding our announcement inside a traditional holiday stocking filled with coal to emphasize the point. Because at Capital Communications, we are not averse to mixing metaphors, blending legends or hurling snowballs of our own when it comes to dramatizing the true meaning of Christmas."

Donte laughed. "You wouldn't."

"Oh, we would and we shall," she replied. "The strategy's from *The Art of War*." There was silence on Donte's end. "Sun Tzu? The Chinese author of the famous military treatise," she added on the presumption he didn't know the source.

"No, I was just thinking of the irony: Citing a Chinese philosopher—at Christmas time."

Graciella murmured, quickly followed by "You wouldn't happen to know where we could buy some coal around here?"

Donte burst out laughing. "You're serious!"

"Dead serious," she assured him.

"Well, it's kinda sparse in these parts. Nothing else, just go with charcoal briquettes—same difference." She laughed. "Hey, I've been working on something, too."

"What's that?" she inquired.

"A sweetener to help make your castor oil go down a little easier."

Graciella giggled. "Oh, we're having too much fun. Tell me more."

Donte shared that he had come up with a simple solution to Stoyonix' need for public credit: he created a back of the card design with the message, *This holiday gift brought to you, in part, by (insert Stoyonix logo)*.

"Brilliant," she gushed. "Now, I've got to run. Got another client meeting at one, and just enough time to eat my salad, and send off this holiday greeting to the Stoyonix Communications VP."

"Sounds great. You'll let us know?"

"Of course," she replied. "And, assuming they see the wisdom of our ways, I've dreamt up an incredible event idea that should make everyone happy. After work would you like to hear about it over dinner?"

The request came out so suddenly, it took him by surprise. "Dinner?"

Alena, who had nearly finished decorating the tree, dropped the twinkling lights to place her hands on both hips to encourage her father to take the offer.

"Sure. . ." he said hesitantly. "Where and when?"

Graciella said she'd make reservations for 7:30 at Mortons. She then read off her cell number. "Just in case you're late." Always the tease, he thought.

* * *

Inside the Soltero workshop, Jamas and Rollie were hunched over a workbench. Jamas was holding the toy wooden wagon from rolling off the table, while his father tapped the back end down in the slots formed by the two side panels. He didn't want to force the rear panel, so he grabbed the sand paper. "These grooves are just a little too tight," the older man noted.

Rolando laid the rear panel of the wagon on the table, and sanded the edge on one side, smoothly and methodically, with the strokes sliding in one direction; always away. As Jamas steadied the table, he admired the dexterity of his father's fingers, especially as they were thick and scarred from years of pounding nails, sawing planks, and mitering wooden joints.

"Little Roy's gonna love this wagon, Dad," Jamas said.

"Oh, yeah. I just hope your little nephew doesn't love it too much," Rollie chuckled. "Would be nice if he kept it in good condition, so maybe he could pass it on to his son one day."

Rollie stopped sanding and slowly looked up into the face of his second son. He wondered if his comment may have been misconstrued, as Jamas likely would never have a biological son of his own. Ever since that day when he announced to his parents that he was a gay man Rolando never talked with Jamas about his sexual orientation. As an old school Portuguese, Rolando had been raised Catholic and grown up to believe that homosexuality was taboo. Throughout his life, nobody in his right mind would ever suggest that marriage could be anything but a commitment between a man and a woman. Despite the enormous guilt he felt inside, he knew one thing: Jamas was a good boy, a pure soul. He loved his son and would never do anything to offend or hurt him.

The bell on the door interrupted their quiet and announced they had a visitor. "Halloo, halloo, Merry Christmas," said the portly woman, closing the door behind her while jangling the bell. She appeared well dressed, affluent, perhaps in her early sixties, Jamas figured. Rollie approached the counter with a quizzical expression. He recognized the woman, but struggled to recall her name, remembering only that it sounded like the name of a famous French movie actor.

"Mr. Soltero," she reached her hand across the counter. "Please tell me you haven't forgotten me! I've been in here twice in the past five years, and purchased Christmas boxes for two of my grandchildren."

The quizzical expression was etched on his face like a Greek mask. At this stage of his life, the name would never pop into his memory.

"Mrs. Hanson LeValier." She spoke the name in a lilting and melodious manner that suggested she'd spent hours rehearsing the pronunciation in front of the grand mirror in the elegantly decorated front room of her Fab Forties mansion. "Like *Chevalier*."

She came in closer to the counter. "Now, I've driven down here today specifically to purchase one of your Christmas boxes for my grandson. What are you calling them this year, 'Wish Holders'?" She glanced inside the case at the wooden objects, searching for confirmation of the new name of the toy. "Is that Cocobolo?" she whispered as if they were suddenly standing inside the church sanctuary.

"No, but you have a good eye," Rollie said. "They're made of Bolivian Rosewood."

"In that case, I'll take three."

Jamas approached the counter. "They're not for sale, ma'am. You may have missed our sign out front."

"My good boy, sale signs are irrelevant to me." She pulled a $100 bill from her purse and slid it across the glass counter. "This is the last weekend of the shopping season, and I mean to get the one that I need today."

"Mrs. LeValier, really." Rolando Soltero shoved the payment back across the counter. "We cannot sell the boxes at this time. I am very sorry. It's a legal matter."

She lowered her voice. "What sort of legal matter? Perhaps I can be of assistance."

Jamas looked at his father, who was scratching the back half of his head, which in the process tilted the hat forward so that it covered his eyes. An intentional gesture, Jamas surmised. "Some corporation is threatening us with an injunction," he told her, "because of a possible trademark infringement."

The woman's mouth dropped. And she immediately dove into her purse once more and pulled out a business card. She handed it to Rolando. "My husband's firm: Merschdorff, Bergman and LeValier. One of the largest corporate law firms in Sacramento. I'll call him the moment I get in my car." She started for the door.

"Mrs. LeValier," Jamas called after her. "Your money!" He waved the bill with Franklin's smile directed at the grand dame's derrière.

"That's a deposit, young man," she said. "You'll hold one of those gorgeous Wish Holders for me, won't you?" She didn't wait for a response, closing the door behind her. The bell echoed in the workshop.

* * *

When Donte turned the corner past the workshop, he saw that all the available parking spaces on the street were taken. The commercial building across 34th Street had leased offices to several companies that entertained drop-in customers. It didn't bother him that he had had to park a block away. Walking toward the workshop, he remembered back five years ago when his father had shown him the dilapidated building and said he and Uncle Rolando were thinking of locating a workshop there. Donte thought he was kidding; the building was condemned and in atrocious condition. But the rent was incredibly cheap, and presented nicely to a well-traveled street with the one large display window. And with the construction knowledge and experience shared by the two brothers and their third partner "Streamy" Madros, they figured to have the place shipshape in ninety days.

They missed by three days, but when Donte had entered the renovated building that fall, he was amazed. All of the plumbing had been replaced. Hardwood floors refinished. The stained stucco walls had all been ripped out, exposing authentic, turn-of-the-century Muddox brickwork that was much too beautiful for a simple crafts workshop. But this place became their second home, as the three men worked casually, at their own pace, in creating custom, hand-crafted children's toys. He mused how Uncle Ricardo, the artist in the family and youngest of the Soltero brothers, would have participated in this group if he hadn't lived so far away, and died so young. In a way, Donte had filled his role.

First the men had started the project as a means of providing their grandchildren with unique, one-of-a-kind Christmas presents. It also allowed them to try out new ideas. Eventually, parents of their grandchildren's playmates inquired about buying directly from the Soltero's Christmas Workshop. Not long after, all of the small children in the family/friends circle had their very own hand-crafted Soltero wooden toys.

In time, Mr. Madros retired due to poor health, and that's when the two brothers invited Donte to join them in embarking on a new venture: To turn their non-profit toy production into a profitable enterprise, with the proceeds donated each year to a charity of their choice. Then, this past fall, the brothers agreed to allow Donte the leadership role. And just a few weeks later, found them embroiled in this Stoyonix mess. As the injunction had prevented them from selling their product they were unable to recoup the ten-thousand plus in materials expenses Donte had charged on his card. The silver lining in all this: he could use the tax write-down to offset the estimated estate tax resulting from his wife's death. Meantime, as he opened the workshop doors, he wondered whether he'd led his father and uncle down a blind alley.

There was no one in the workshop. Rollie and Jamas apparently had cleaned up the shop and gone off. With work completed on the Christmas Holders, there wasn't anything to do, except for Rollie's personal project for his grandson. Donte found his father sitting inside the conference room reading the newspaper at the table

"Where's Uncle Rollie? I planned to update you both on the Stoyonix situation."

Ernest looked him straight in the eye. "Son, your uncle's gone off to talk. . . to an attorney."

"What?" Donte plopped down in a chair as if to recover from a punch in the stomach. "Pop, do you know that Grace's staff is driving around town right now, looking for coal?"

His father didn't bother to ask. "Should be meeting with him right about now, in fact."

"Damn."

"Your uncle's financial situation is serious, Donnie. He couldn't sit here and wait for you two to figure things out. I tried to talk him out of it." Ernest rose up and patted his son on the back. "You'll lock up, won't ya son."

The bell on the door signaled it was a new ballgame.

CHAPTER FIVE

When he arrived home, Donte smelled kielbasa sausage frying on the stove. He reminded Alena that he would be going out for dinner. She had remembered, nodding at him while browning the meat.

"Your brother home?"

"Nah, he's out shopping with a friend. Should be home soon."

Donte went into his bedroom and opened his closet. He stood there for several minutes debating on which color scheme to wear, and which style would be appropriate for the restaurant. He knew Graciella would come dressed smart and classy, and she expected the same of her date. Date, he chuckled. *Don't fool yourself; to her, it's just another business meeting.* He chose a powder blue Oxford shirt and a pair of gray slacks and laid them on his valet next to the bed. He hung his navy blue blazer on the door and checked the clock: 6:15. He figured he had time for a quick nap before his shower.

Nearly an hour later, Donte entered the family room and surprised Alena, who was sitting on the couch, watching an episode of *Friends*. She looked up and her eyes widened like royalty had entered the room. She blew a long and comedic whistle, and punctuated her approval with a dramatic thumbs up gesture.

"Alright, alright," he said laughing. "Your brother's not home yet?"

"Nope. Still out," she said.

"Well, I'll be at Mortons and I'll have my phone on, if you need me." He turned to leave and said goodnight.

"Have a good time," she called after him.

Walking toward the garage door, he gave a slight wave, a sardonic gesture that he would do his best.

* * *

Among the three of them, Alena appeared to be handling Maria's death better than her brother, and certainly her father. Her mother's untimely passing came at the end of Alena's senior year in high school, casting a pall over final exams and then commencement ceremonies. She didn't even think about going to the "all-night grad party," as her heart just wasn't into it, coming so soon after burying her mother in the ground.

She worked that summer at a retail store in the mall, and mostly stayed home at night, reading. Before she knew it, classes were starting at Sonoma State. And she looked forward to the new experience to cleanse the morbidity surrounding the Soltero household.

When she prepared to leave home that summer morning for the two-hour drive toward the coast, her dad hugged her, kissed her on the cheek and wished her well before she got into the car. While fastening the seat belt, she imagined how, if her mother had been alive, she would not have allowed Alena to just jump in the car and drive away, like she was merely driving off to work. No, Maria would have been hovering around the driver's window, coaxing a few more goodbyes out of her, and issuing reminders that they'd covered many times over inside the house in the days leading up to her departure. As she backed out of the driveway, and watched her father waving goodbye, while biting his lip to keep from crying, she realized how much she missed her mother in moments like these. And how much she'd grown up in the six long months since she had kissed her mother goodbye for the very last time.

* * *

Driving up Interstate 5, Donte was juggling how to reveal the news about his uncle's decision to meet with an attorney. Graciella had already put a lot of time into this project, and he could see her jumping right in to the conversation during hors d'oeuvres, regaling him with exploits about stuffing Christmas stockings with charcoal, while illustrators worked on Grinch-like cartoons in the background. He needed to deliver the disappointing news at the perfect moment.

His memory immediately flew back to that night in the pizza parlor during their senior year when Grace sensed that something was wrong, even in the din of the music blaring from the corner jukebox. She thought he'd been acting strangely those last few days of their high school career. And on that night she wanted to clear the air, so she took Donte outside, away from the partying atmosphere.

Driving up the interstate, Donte could see her reaching for his hand just out of range of the pizza parlor's flashing red neon sign, asking "What's wrong? Just tell me. Whatever it is, we can handle it." He reached out and her long lithe hand slipped into his right palm so easily and perfectly, which made the confession that much harder.

Donte had secretly hoped that she would change her mind, and attend school that fall with him at Sacramento State. But he knew it would be foolish for her to turn down an opportunity to attend UCLA. In a nutshell, he couldn't see how they could continue "as a couple" in a long distance relationship. Not over four years. She thought he was being selfish and short sighted. When he drove her home that night, he knew things would never go back to being what they were; they had chartered a new direction.

About a mile before the downtown exit, his phone rang. His heart sank a little, as he imagined it might be Graciella calling to postpone the dinner; it surprised him how much he was looking forward to this. Instead, it was Alena. He pushed the "talk" button and before he could open with "hello" his daughter yelled "Dad—*Anthony'sbeeninanaccident*. He's hurt bad."

"What? Where?"

"They took him in an ambulance to the Emergency Room at the UC Med Center. I'm leaving now."

"Okay, honey. Don't worry. I'll meet you there." Before he pushed the "end" button, he mustered his steeliest calm voice and said, "Drive safe."

He got off at the downtown exit and pulled his truck over to the curb. He clumsily scrolled through his phone's address book and when it came to "Grace" pushed the button twice. Her phone rang three times before she picked up.

"Hi there." Her voice sounded soothing and sexy. "The waiter just served my Grey Goose marti. . ."

"Anthony's been in a car accident." He hated to be abrupt, but now was not the time for pleasantries. "Alena just called me."

"Oh, no. Is be hurt badly?"

"Don't know yet. But I'm heading over to the Med Center Emergency Room right away."

"I understand." Her voice instantly reverted to the cool, professional calm.

"Thanks." He thought the conversation was over and began to pull the phone away from his ear when he heard her voice call out faintly.

"Donte..."

"Yeah."

"Want me to meet you there? You know, so you have somebody..."

"No," he said firmly. "I mean, that's thoughtful, but Alena's going to meet me there." He could hear the tremor in his own voice. The shock was setting in. "I gotta go."

"Understood," she said.

As he pulled the phone away from his ear he thought he heard her voice say "Drive safe."

* * *

As he emerged through the entrance of the Emergency Room, hospital gurneys rolled past Donte in both directions. He watched an attendant wheeling a patient with his head wrapped in gauze, and it suddenly struck him: he had never stepped into an emergency room before this night.

Alena came running up to her father and embraced him.

"How's Anthony. What do we know?"

Her eyes brimming with tears, she said, "They won't tell me anything. Except that he's in surgery."

Donte immediately marched to the main nurse's station, told them who he was and asked about the status of his son.

"He was the driver of the vehicle?" one nurse asked, looking at a chart.

Donte didn't know. He looked to Alena, who nodded. "He took my car." Donte nodded in reply to the nurse.

"Sir, your son has been badly injured. He slammed into the steering wheel, and he's beat up pretty bad. He's in surgery now. When we know more, we'll have one of the doctors come find you."

"But, did he. . . "

"Sir, that's all we know at this time." She looked at him with an implacable, blank expression. The conversation was over. "You may have a seat in our waiting room."

Alena pulled at her father's jacket sleeve, "C'mon, Dad," leading him toward an empty bench in the waiting area.

He took a seat in silence with his daughter. Looking around the room, he stared at the other men and women; some younger, some older sitting there with worn, expressionless faces also dealing with the uncertainty of their loved ones.

"Had he been drinking?" Donte said quietly into his clasped hands resting below him.

"I don't know," Alena responded quietly.

"Tell me the truth."

"I don't know!" she shouted at him.

"Who was he out with tonight? That Billy kid?"

Alena voice returned to a quiet hush. "Think so."

Donte looked around the room for Mr. Maxwell. He had met him once, last year, when both fathers arrived in the school parking lot believing it was their turn to pick up the kids from the dance. *Mr. Maxwell was an okay guy*, Donte remembered, *an executive with one of the bottling companies. Or was it a liquor firm?* Maybe there was hope for Billy after all, but Donte couldn't see that far in the future. Looking around the Waiting Room, he didn't see Maxwell anywhere, and wondered if Billy had already been discharged.

He noticed that the hospital had tried to appropriately decorate for the season, but Donte only observed cheap, chintzy red bows and that fake, stiff green stuff they drape over doorways to simulate boughs of evergreens. He wondered, *why is it accidents always seem to hit you, right at the holidays?* Donte got up from his seat, leaned over and whispered to his daughter. "I'm going out for a smoke. I can't sit here right now." She started to follow. "No, you stay here, 'Lena. In case, they call for us." Alena didn't want to be alone again. Ever.

Outside in the cold, brisk night air, Donte lit up a cigar and edged away from the entrance to avoid the many "NO SMOKING" signs. He walked around the corner of the building where the smoke wouldn't bother anyone and it was quieter.

He started to pray for his son, but thought better of it while standing there, smoking a stogie, thinking those looking down from the heavens might view it as a gesture of disrespect. As his mind began to quiet, he thought how this could be one of those life-changing moments, when you look back and realize the world had been heading down a comfortable, well-worn path, and then fate abruptly tosses you in a ditch, and suddenly that becomes your new permanent path. His heart sank at the thought. "God, no, please. Don't take my son," he prayed quietly.

Little Anthony. Named for Ernesto's father, Antonio Soltero, from some little town in Brazil, his little boy had taken the larger chunk of Donte's soul. He loved Alena immensely, that was a given. And she loved him back far more than Anthony had ever shown up to this point. *Granted, he's only sixteen.* But in the process of raising his younger child, he had invested more of his heart and soul in the little boy. As this was his second turn in parenting, during infancy he was less resistant to changing poopy diapers, or getting up for midnight bottle feedings. Parental requirements didn't seem to chafe as much in the raising of little Anthony. He took him to his doctor visits, dental appointments and always seemed to be the one who took time off from work to race to the school for the unplanned parent-teacher conference when Anthony had gotten into a schoolyard scrape or clogged the boy's room toilet by flushing another student's jacket.

And then there were all the soccer and baseball games he had personally driven his son to (not to mention those boring practices), while his wife Maria was off doing much the same with their daughter, Alena. The woman had taken responsibility for the daughter and the man the son. It was the way things were supposed to be, especially when the children, especially the daughter, entered puberty. Donte couldn't imagine himself trying to prepare young Alena for "the talk." With Anthony, he felt he could share almost anything, as he thought of him as his best buddy for life. He stomped the cigar on the concrete curb, and bent down to pick up the stub, silently praying once more, "Please, God. Don't take my Anthony from me."

The sound of approaching voices startled him. Two men came around the corner from the nearest building, and in the cold quiet stillness, their voices echoed throughout the courtyard. One presumably was a doctor, as he was wearing a white smock, and the other, an attendant in greens. When they spoke, he could see their breath in the cold night air.

"It's something, alright. I'd call it a miracle," the attendant said.

"I don't know if I'd go that far," said the doctor. "I don't know what to call it. Young woman, stage four pancreatic cancer, less than a week to go. Suddenly. . . completely healed. Maybe it is a miracle."

When they approached, Donte turned to let them pass. "I'd say it was a 'Rigl miracle'," the attendant said, prompting a one-burst laugh from the doctor over the clever wordplay.

Although Donte didn't understand the pun shared between the two professionals, somewhere in the back of his mind a tiny bell was ringing in the distance. It stopped abruptly when Donte looked down the street and saw the silhouette of a thick-chested man ambling up the sidewalk, walking with a septuagenarian hustle. Donte walked down to meet Ernest by the entrance.

"How did you. . . " Donte sputtered.

"Graciella called me," Ernest barked. "Thought I should know. And to be sure a grownup was lookin' after ya." Done lecturing his son, he asked, "How's the boy?"

"Don't know yet. He's in surgery."

"Is it bad?" he asked, climbing toward the entrance.

"They don't know, Dad. He's *in* surgery." Donte let the fact speak for itself.

"Where's Alena?"

"She's inside." Donte led the way through the double sets of automatic doors. When they were in the Waiting Area, he turned back toward his father. "Dad, who's the guy from Stoyonix who sent you that warning letter."

Ernest glanced past his son, looking for his granddaughter. "Regal something. Or reale. I don't know. Why?"

"Curious," Donte said, leading him to where Alena was sitting around the corner.

Alena stood and hugged her grandfather. Ernest patted her on the back, reassuring her. "There, there, now. Don't worry, darlin'. Everything's going to be alright."

Ernest sat down in the middle of the bench. Alena sat on his right and Donte on the opposite side. They sat quietly for less than a minute. Then Ernest suddenly bobbed his head and said with conviction, "C'mon. We start praying."

"You mean like the 'Our Father'?" Alena asked.

"No, darlin', you pray to specific saints in time of need. Like Saint Jude is patron saint of lost causes." Suddenly, a look of shock began to spread over his granddaughter's face. "No, that's just an example." Alena was relieved.

"Alright," Ernest continued, grabbing his granddaughter's hand, "now you pray to Saint Nicholas."

"You mean Santa Claus?"

"Saint *NICHOLAS*," Ernest corrected her. "Patron saint of children."

He reached out to grab his son's hand, but Donte had anticipated the gesture and already tucked his hand underneath his coat. "Uh, you pray for. . . oh, what is the patron saint of illnesses, injuries." Ernest rose from the bench, in a look of confusion. "Oh, I shoulda memorized that list of saints in catechism."

He hurried over to the nurse's station. He asked the first attendant who looked up, "Do you happen to know who the patron saint of injuries is?"

"No, I'm sorry. This is not a Catholic hospital, sir."

He gave her a curt, dismissive wave and returned to the children. Standing in front of his son, his foot was tapping as his mind raced.

"Still searchin' the old childhood memories, huh?" Donte enjoyed kidding his father in times like these. It served as a brief diversion from the potentially stark reality facing them at this moment. But Ernest appeared to have delved deep into his subconscious for the memory.

"*Rita!*" Ernest gushed, throwing his hands apart in a moment of discovery. "Pray to Saint Rita."

"What does she do?"

Ernest nervously rolled his hands in small circles. "Patron saint of injuries, healing of wounds, that sort of thing."

Donte couldn't help but smile at his father. "And, how did you recall that arcane bit of Catholic trivia."

"Because in school, there was this girl—Rita—a sweet, little freckle-faced redheaded girl, Scottish last name I can't remember. And some of us boys would tease her, we used to run up to her and say, 'Saint Rita, please heal my wounds.' And then we'd pucker up our lips, as if we wanted her to kiss us. Ahh, Rita," he grinned. "Rita McIverson, that was it!"

Alena looked up in astonishment. "Grandpa—that's mean."

"Oh, no, darlin', it was just. . . being kids."

Ernest's eyes suddenly grew large, as if he'd seen a ghost. Anthony entered the room and stood next to his grandfather as casual as a kid who had just come home from the fishing hole. The boy had a gauze pad over his right eye, and his right arm was in a sling.

Alena and Donte rushed toward him, forming a group hug in the process. "Oww, go easy," Anthony bellowed at his sister. "My arm."

Donte pulled everyone away. "They told us you were in surgery. Are you alright?"

"Yeah, I'm alright. No, I wasn't in surgery," Anthony said weakly. "They were talking about Billy. He's still there."

Donte and Alena were stunned. *What part of the story had they gotten so wrong?* "Were you driving?" Alena asked.

"No, Billy was. I was on the passenger side."

"But you're okay?" his father confirmed.

"Yeah, except for a bruised shoulder. And this cut over my eye. I banged the side door pretty hard." Donte laid his right arm around his son's neck and hugged him.

"Have they contacted Mr. Maxwell, do you know?"

"He's still out of town, at a convention and won't get here 'til midnight, I guess. That's what I heard."

A nurse attendant approached the family and informed Donte of his son's minor injuries. She also handed him the wallet found inside the car. Donte opened it and immediately noticed the driver's license: William Q. Maxwell. "No, this isn't his. It's the other boy's," Donte told her. He looked at his daughter and together they shared an "ah-ha" moment.

The nurse reached for a second bag of personal effects, waded through it and pulled out a wallet that read Anthony J. Soltero on the license. "Sorry for the mix up. You folks must have been sick with worry. We're so sorry."

"That's fine, it turned out okay." Donte interrupted her. "How's the Maxwell boy?"

"Well, he's lost a fair amount of blood. And he's got several internal injuries. He's in serious condition. But he should come out of it. Would you like us to let you know when he gets out of surgery?"

"Yes, please." Donte jotted down his phone number for her. "Any time, please call."

Donte looked up and saw Grandpa Ernesto escorting his two grandchildren out of the Emergency Room toward the parking lot.

CHAPTER SIX

The next morning around 9:30, Donte arrived at Grace's midtown office unannounced. He could see her entire staff sitting around the conference room table, with Grace chairing the meeting. A young woman got up to greet him and said that they were just finishing and should be done in less than ten minutes. She said Grace asked if he would please wait. She invited him to the coffee on the table and returned to her staff meeting.

In the lobby waiting area, with coffee in hand, Donte wound his way to the wall covered with news articles about Grace's rise to PR fame: Ms. Sacramento Business Woman of the Year, the *Sacramento Business Journal* List of Top 25 PR Firms, showing Capital Communications in third place with more than $1.6 million in billings and dozens of photographs where she posed with the mayor, the governor and many other high-powered business types who appeared at special events coordinated by her firm. Donte was highly impressed. As a graphic designer in the advertising market, he had always heard her firm was a bona fide "player," but never dreamed she had attained the upper echelon in the market.

When Grace came out to greet him, she immediately asked about Anthony's medical status. Donte explained he was home and doing all right. As she escorted him into her private office, she apologized about being too forward in offering to "be there for him." He shrugged casually, and said that she really should be apologizing for calling Ernesto and dispatching him to the Emergency Room. His smile told her he wasn't upset about that either.

"*Whew*, what a week," she exclaimed. "So, where does that leave us?" The upward rise in her voice at the end of the sentence suggested an optimism that belied the direness of the situation. Donte took a deep breath as he figured there was no better time than the present to tell her the discouraging news about his uncle enlisting the services of a local attorney. While he paused to collect his thoughts, she stole his thunder.

"*I* have news," she said. "*Great* news, in fact. Stoyonix emailed me this morning, and agreed to our terms. *All* of them. We can donate the Christmas Wish Holders to the orphanage." Graciella's hands were pressed together with the ebullient anticipation of a game show contestant awaiting the opening of door number three. "Can you freakin' believe that?"

Donte couldn't be more stunned than if he'd been stung by a manta ray. "Seriously."

"Yep, they've agreed to a special event to be held at the orphanage next Tuesday—mark your calendar—where we'll make the presentation before all the media. They're sending their president Ronko Stoyonovich, their head legal guy, and. . . "

". . . can't believe this. . . "

". . . best yet—they've agreed to work with us in turning the event into an on-air fundraiser so that Soltero brothers won't have to come up with the cash donation you had committed."

"I'm amazed," he said. Christmas had come early.

"Actually, the best part is we won't have to go out and buy fifteen bags of charcoal briquettes." Her devious smile lit up the entire room. "Aren't you excited? I'm positively elated," she said, throwing her arms in the air, punctuated by a touchdown-scoring *Whoohoooohh!* "So, what was your news?"

Donte admitted it seemed anti-climactic now. He explained how his uncle had "hired" an attorney to oversee the infringement suit.

"Well, I hope he doesn't take credit for our good work yesterday!" Grace then remembered there was one stipulated condition: Stoyonix wished to receive partial credit for making the donation possible, and wanted to take them up on the offer to imprint their logo on the back of the Wish cards.

Donte casually reached into his notebook and pulled out the dummy prototype of the card, with the Wish instructions on front, and the Stoyonix credit line on the back. He had even printed their logo in their corporate cobalt blue color.

"Nice," Graciella said. "Looks like the framework's in place. Now, we just have to make sure your father and uncle don't have anything planned for next Tuesday night."

"They're good; I'm pretty sure."

"Then, we can get started planning this puppy. And we have to start right away." She checked her schedule on the Droid. "Any chance you might want to join me for dinner tonight?" She realized she was being extremely forward again, but as she had learned long ago, if you don't go for what you want, no one is going to hand it to you. "This will give you a chance to make up for that broken date last night," she kidded him.

"Actually. . . " he allowed the word to hang in the air for dramatic effect, "I'd better not." Her face lost a little of its confident glow. "Anthony's still pretty banged up, and I just can't leave him tonight," Donte admitted.

"Oh, of course," she said. "How stupid of me."

Donte smiled in acknowledgement. "So, for that reason, we're going to have to reverse the invitation and ask *you* to join *us* for a home cooked meal instead." He saw the glow return to her lovely face. "Say, seven-ish?"

* * *

The doorbell rang. Alena carefully laid the wine glasses down on the table. "I'll get it," she yelled loud enough so that her father could hear over the noise of the fan above the stove where boiling pasta steamed the kitchen. She opened the door and greeted Graciella, who was holding a bottle of Merlot against her valise.

"Hello. So nice to meet you." Her pleasant smile instantly ingratiated her with the college student. While Alena helped the older woman slip out of her overcoat, Donte entered the foyer with an apron tied around his waist and a towel over his shoulder. "Look at the master chef."

Once again, Grace had properly dressed for the occasion: alabaster white knit sweater with cocoa-colored pants, low heeled black loafers. Even in casual wear, she appeared stunning. As Alena hung the coat in the closet, Donte was struck by how closely his daughter resembled his friend. Both were tall, about 5'9", dark brown hair down to their shoulders and smiles that could light a darkened fireplace. Graciella gave Donte a polite embrace and quickly released as she knew the daughter would be observing.

"Great place you have here!" Grace said, looking around the formal dining area. "How long have you lived here?'"

Donte did the mental calculation in his memory by replaying scenes of Anthony as a toddling infant when they had moved into this home. "About fifteen years."

Grace held out the bottle of Merlot. "Wasn't sure what you were serving, but this is great any time."

Donte led them into the living room area, adjacent to the kitchen. Anthony was sitting alone on the couch, his right arm healing in a sling, watching Sports Center. When his father introduced the woman, Anthony lifted his left arm and politely shook hands, although it felt awkward.

Graciella looked around and soaked in the accoutrements that fostered the wonderfully warm and 'homey' atmosphere: family portraits above the hearth, pictures of both sets of grandparents, along with individual photos of Alena in her soccer uniform, and Anthony in his Little League uniforms, bat in hand, and silly grins that always emerge when a young boy is commanded to "smile" at the count of three.

"Still play?" she turned to Anthony, who nodded politely. "What position?"

"Pitcher and infield."

Over the din of the kitchen fan, Donte offered "This year, he's slated to be one of the team's starting pitchers. Just a junior."

"Yeah, soon as my arm heals," he said, lifting the sling for the woman's attention.

Grace had deftly avoided mentioning the accident, as she didn't want to appear like an interrogating old aunt. But now that he had opened the door, it provided an opportunity. "Pretty bad accident, huh." She sat down next to him on the couch.

Anthony repeated the scenario his father had related earlier that morning in her office. Bruised right shoulder and small laceration above the eye. Both injuries should be healed in time for the beginning of the baseball season.

"You go to many River Cats' games?" she asked about the local Triple-A baseball club. The boy nodded. "I have some contacts there; maybe could get you in to see batting practice sometime—on the field. Meet some of the players. Would you like that?"

Anthony's eyes widened, allowing her to notice his light brown eyes for the first time. "You bet!"

Graciella smiled. "I'll let your dad know. And we'll set it up." She rose from the couch, and sat on a bar stool, facing into the kitchen. "So, what's on the menu tonight, Chef Soltero?"

Donte was in the act of draining the pasta into the calendar in the sink, while steam swirled up and around his face. "That would be homemade sauce over spaghetti noodles with a world-class salad and French bread."

"And the Merlot."

"And good red wine," he added.

"If it's any good, can I have the recipe?"

Donte slammed the metal pot on the kitchen counter tile for comedic effect. "Yeah, but then I'd have to. . . "

". . . I know, you'd have to kill me," she finished the line, laughing.

Minutes later they were sitting around the dining room table enjoying the fine home cooked meal. Donte had poured full glasses of the Merlot for the adults and small amounts for both kids. He had been raised in a household where wine was always served with meals, and the older children were allowed to consume small quantities. Which is one of the reasons Donte believed there were no alcoholics in his family. It was a theory.

During dinner, however, he found himself carefully guarded and moving in awkwardly formal movements, despite the effects of the wine. It was all due to the fact that a lovely, strange woman was dining with them for the first time since. . . well, ever. He watched her responding to the children with such effortless charm, and realized she had been aptly named "Grace." As the candle light from the table shone on her face, illuminating her sparkling cocoa-colored eyes, for a moment it triggered a flickering memory of their passionate teenage love. His reverie was interrupted when Grace asked Alena about college life and whether she had declared a major.

"Probably interior design, but I'm not sure yet. I'm just a freshman."

"Really? Interior design. That's what I wanted to major in when I went to UCLA. Instead, I chickened out and went for communications." Grace hoisted her glass in a mock gesture to success.

Donte studied her carefully, his mind wandering back to the dark recesses of his youth. "I don't remember that." He watched her respond with a slight shoulder shrug as she sipped her wine. "How could I not know that?"

Not wanting to rehash that part of their past, when Donte had sent a letter to her at UCLA spelling out all the reasons why their relationship could not stand the differences in geography and culture, and declared them officially "broken up," Grace shifted the conversation to the previous night's accident.

"How is the other boy doing?"

She was informed that Billy came out of surgery with a positive prognosis. He would remain in the hospital for a few days.

"Anthony, one thing about the accident that is curious to me. . . how was it that the hospital mistook you for the other boy?"

"Well, Billy was driving his mother's car," Anthony said, laying his fork on the plate with his left hand. He explained that when the emergency medical team arrived on the scene, they had found Billy's wallet on the bench seat and his wallet down on the floor of the driver's side.

Donte interrupted, "Well, how did your wallet end up there?"

"We'd gone for burgers earlier at Jack-in-the-Box," the boy told his father. "And when I paid, I put my wallet between the windshield and the dashboard. Billy left his on the seat. When we collided with the other car, my wallet must have slid across the dash and fell over on the driver's side floorboard."

"And these boys almost look like identical twins, same color hair. . . " Donte offered. The two adults shared glances they were satisfied with the explanation. Mystery solved.

After the kids had left the table—Anthony went into his bedroom, while Alena dutifully washed the dishes—Donte informed Graciella that he had called a family meeting for 9 o'clock the next morning at the workshop. "I didn't tell them the news. I'll save the surprise announcement for you."

"Well, thank you."

"After all, it was your good work that got us here." The compliment succeeded in generating a warm smile from the PR pro and the perfect chance to deliver his punch line. "And my brilliant performance that set it up," he said, tapping the side of his forehead. Grace tossed her napkin across the table, where it was blocked by the chandelier. They broke up laughing like school kids.

For the next hour, they collaborated on the concept of a Christmas-oriented special event, featuring the dedication of the Christmas Wish holders to the orphanage children. Grace explained that Stoyonix would bring the oversized check in the amount of $5,000 to kick-start the fundraising drive. Donte could tell that Graciella had impeccable taste in selecting the most appropriate items to stage the backdrop so that it would communicate the desired message concisely and effectively, with just the right touch of panache.

* * *

When they were done, Donte walked Graciella outside in the chilly night air. She popped open the passenger's side door of her Jaguar with the key-remote and placed her valise on the seat. "Oh, that was a great meal, Mr. Soltero. You're a good cook."

Donte shrugged modestly, taking the compliment in stride. She opened her arms to invite a friendly hug. As they embraced, Donte expected the same polite brief hug he received when she had entered the house. Instead, the embrace evolved into a long, robust squeeze, like a sustained note from Benny Goodman's clarinet.

"You feel so good," she whispered in his ear, clutching him close.

He responded, "You, too." He felt her arms begin to relinquish the embrace, then gradually gripping tighter again.

"I don't want to let you go," she said.

He thought he heard sniffling. He drew away to check. "Are you. . . crying?"

"A little," she said, whisking tears from her right cheek.

"Why?"

"It's silly."

Donte's smile invited her to try. He pulled away a few inches more to closely examine her almond-shaped eyes, now more beautiful than ever, as they glistened in the crystal cold evening. He realized they were revealing something profound.

"You have what I always wanted," she said.

His facial response revealed disbelief. "You were married, for what, four years?"

"Three. I know. It's crazy," she said, wiping the last tears from her cheek. "But I never stopped loving you. At least a little. And now. . . "

"Now. . . " he wondered where that left them as things seemed to be charging forward at lightning speed.

"Here we are. . . suddenly back together again," she blurted in a nervous laugh. "Oh, I'm sorry. . . "

"It's just. . . "

She sensed his discomfort. "I know. . . "

". . . so soon after Maria. . . you know."

Grace realized she had overplayed her position, and patted him on the shoulder with a friendly gesture. "I know." She kissed him lightly on the cheek, walked around to the driver's side, and crouched to enter the car. She waved once through the windshield to reassure him everything was fine, despite the fist-sized knot she felt in her stomach.

He watched the taillights growing distant as the Jaguar retreated down the street. A brisk breeze caused him to shiver. Or was it the suddenness of this new relationship, he wondered, that appeared to be blooming in the dark depths of a cold winter night. And felt so amazingly perfect.

Probably, too perfect.

CHAPTER SEVEN

The next morning, Donte arrived at the workshop three minutes past nine. Yet when he entered the conference room, the table was laden with plates of still-warm croissants from La Bou pastry shop. Graciella was serving coffee from the portable carafe she'd brought in with the pastries. She looked up with an inviting smile. "Coffee?"

"Please." Donte saw that Uncle Rolando had already eaten one half of his almond croissant, and his father was tearing into one.

"Can you believe this girl, Donnie?" Ernie enthused. "She brings coffee and pastry in the morning."

Donte sensed an immediate thaw in the air, a warmness that hadn't been there ever since Stoyonix Corporation sent the threatening letter.

"Where's Jimmie?"

Uncle Rolando swallowed and washed it down with a thick slurp of coffee. "Surfing."

"You've gotta be kidding!" Donte said. "In this weather. He's crazy."

"Weatherman's calling for snow—did you hear this—on Christmas Eve," Ernest told the group. "When's the last time you can remember it snowin' on Christmas, Rollie?"

The older man brushed croissant crumbs from his jacket. "Hell, I can't recall what I had for breakfast yesterday. How do you expect me to remember that?" Grace giggled.

"Oh, tomorrow, you'll remember what you had for breakfast yesterday, I'll guarantee you that." Ernest slapped his brother on the back. The group laughed at Uncle Rolando, who played the role of curmudgeon wonderfully. When the laughter died down, Ernesto looked at Donte and then Graciella. "So, you kids have good news for us, I hope? Otherwise, I doubt you'd be serving us these lovely, fattening pastries."

"We do," admitted Grace cheerfully. She wiped her mouth on a napkin, and pulled the email from Stoyonix Corporation from her valise. "Mr. Soltero," she said to Ernest, ". . . and Mr. Soltero," she directed at Uncle Rollie, ". . . your presence is requested this Tuesday evening at the Saint Celestin's Orphanage at 6:30 p.m., where you will present—along with officials from Stoyonix Corporation—your Christmas Wish Holders to the orphanage administrator and several of her children . . . on live TV."

Rolando looked over at his brother, shrugged his shoulder slightly while exhibiting a half-hearted expression.

Graciella continued, ". . . and, where Mr. Ronko Stoyonovich, Stoyonix company president, will kick off a fundraising drive throughout the greater Sacramento area, the proceeds of which will benefit the orphanage." She looked at the older men, but read in their faces a less than satisfactory response. Grace looked at Donte to see if he was reading the situation the same way. He was and took up the baton.

"Dad, Uncle Rollie. . . this is what we wanted. We negotiated a peace settlement with the Visigoths for criminy sakes. C'mon, what's the matter with you guys?"

They watched the older men glance over at each other, expressionless, once more. Then, Uncle Rollie's lips tightened, ever so slightly, and his eyes began to squint. And, as Ernest was watching closely, he snickered in response. Soon, the two men roared with laughter, while Ernest pounded the table with absolute glee.

"What the hell?" Donte looked at Graciella, who was equally dumbfounded.

"We. . . hehehehe. . . we. . . hehhehheh, we kne. . . that's old news!" roared Ernest, clutching his stomach with convulsive laughter. "That's old news."

"Ancient news," Uncle Rollie chimed in. The brothers roared again at the wordplay displayed by the mild-mannered older brother. As their laughs subsided, Rolando wiped his eyes with his handkerchief, and then blew his nose on it.

"What the hell do you mean 'old news'?" Donte asked in a playfully demanding voice.

Ernest explained that last night Rolando had received a call from Mr. LeValier, the attorney. "Darlin'," he said to Grace, "I don't know if this big lug ever told you, but my brother here sought the advice of an attorney this week."

Graciella nodded, still showing a half-smile from

the resounding laughter echoing in her ears. "He mentioned it."

"LeValier had called Rolando last night to inform him that the Legal Counsel from Stoyonix, that Bernard Rigl, had phoned that they wanted to drop the whole thing. That they had reread your paper and came to the conclusion—'tis the season, an' all—that it would be in the best interests of everyone involved, especially the little tykes at the orphanage, that they drop the whole thing. They gave in on every single point.

"And, best yet. . . "

Graciella cut in ". . . they're gonna help us raise the twelve grand on live TV."

"That's right," Ernest slapped his hands. "So, when we say 'old news,' trust us, we slept very well last night knowing this matter had been settled."

"And still, you allowed this poor kid," Donte said, pointing toward Grace, "to serve you guys coffee and donuts."

"Yes, and it was damn delicious, too," Ernest roared and pounded the table once more.

Graciella closed her valise. "Good. And you boys can clean up." She rose from the table for dramatic effect.

Ernest laughed again. "Happy to, darlin'."

Donte escorted Graciella out the door and wished her a pleasant weekend. She reminded him it would be a "working weekend," as she had to write a plan for her staff, which would be coming in tomorrow—Sunday—to start implementing the action points. "Lots to do before our big event on Tuesday." Graciella asked Donte to forward an electronic version of the artwork for the card, and they would arrange for the printing. He promised he would.

She leaned in for a hug, but anticipating an uneasy moment, smiled. "Short and friendly. I promise." When she released the embrace, she walked directly to the Jag, started the vehicle and drove off.

* * *

As Donte watched her motor down 34th Street, Ernesto came out of the workshop, closed the door behind him and punched his son's arm. "Got ya good, that time, eh?"

"Sure did." His father, zipped his winter coat, said goodbye and began walking around the corner, heading for home.

"Dad, you need a lift?"

"Lift? It's only four blocks."

"It's pretty cold. C'mon, I'll drive you home." The older man agreed, and got in his son's Dodge truck. Donte made the right turn on Folsom Boulevard. As it was a short drive away, he got to the point. "Pop, who is that attorney from Stoyonix?"

"Bernard Rigl," the father said. "That's how the attorney pronounced it anyways, like 'get real'. Why?"

Donte scratched his chin. "The other night, when you found me outside the Emergency Room at the hospital..."

"... yeah."

"I had just overheard something interesting." He told his father about the conversation between the doctor and attendant and how they laughed that perhaps it was a "Rigl miracle." Donte explained it was a play on words.

Ernest hunched his shoulders. "So?"

"Well, don't you see?" The father admitted he couldn't make the connection. "This is the same attorney who bailed on our meeting last week, they told us, because he had 'a family medical situation' to attend to in the Valley." Donte pulled up next to the curb in front of the Soltero home.

"Sorry, son. Still not following ya," the old man said releasing his seatbelt.

Donte turned toward his father. "I think this man believes his daughter is free from cancer because he wrote a wish on the card and dropped it in the Holder that we left there for them."

The father looked over and shook his head. "I dunno. Takes a whole lotta prayin' for that kind of miracle, son." He got out of the truck and walked up the driveway. When the old man had entered the house the son drove off, still wondering if it was prayer or shamanic meditation that miraculously healed the woman.

Or both.

* * *

Over the next two days, Donte and Graciella exchanged a few email messages. It started when he sent over the graphic design of the Wish card. She replied that her staff designer needed to make a setting adjustment to the RGB color palette to achieve the desired cobalt hue of the Stoyonix logo. Donte had no problem with the change, but it reinforced his long held suspicion that his skills were deteriorating, as the world of graphic design, Internet web design and technology in general was changing so rapidly one could no longer expect to stay current professionally with a lifelong subscription to an industry trade publication.

On Tuesday morning, the day of the dedication, waiting in his email in-basket was a message from Grace wishing him a "Happy Winter Solstice" in the subject line. He thought that was odd, but understood that some people take pleasure in wishing friends and relatives a happy day on special occasions that border on silly. Saint Valentine Day, for example, was one he could do without.

For Donte Soltero, Saint Valentine Day represented an unwritten requirement that a fellow is expected to run out and buy a box of chocolates and pick up a dozen roses for his "Valentine," and pity the poor fool who fails on either front by coming home empty handed. He understood implicitly that females everywhere would chafe at such heresy, but Donte thought it was downright silly to demarcate a specific date when he felt one must exhibit their feelings for a true love, when one should actively display that love on a monthly, weekly, or in some cases, daily basis, depending on the situation. Similarly, one should not be coerced to run out at the same late afternoon hour with a dozen other poor shlubs who were lucky enough to remember to shop for the obligatory candy/flowers before the witching hour, lest they arrive home empty handed, only to be greeted by the flat side of an iron skillet by an emotionally wounded 'Valentine.'

Then it suddenly hit him: in just six weeks, he would have no one to share Valentine's Day with for the very first time in many years. *Aww, hell with it*, he thought.

As he read through the "Happy Winter Solstice" message, Donte assumed that Graciella had attempted to connect with him on a back-to-the-earth, rainforesty level. He suspected she had never before wished anyone a greeting on the Winter Solstice, but had selected this opportunity and this vehicle to improve their communication. Worked for him. He felt sure that if he wrote back that the actual translation of the word "solstice" meant "sun stands still," she would unequivocally brand him a pagan sun worshipper and likely never speak to him again, so he erased that message from his "draft" basket and went out for a cigar smoke.

Later, he replied to the message, asking if all the preparations for the evening's big event were nailed down? He offered his services, and asked if he could be of assistance? She replied that there were still dozens of loose ends, normal on the day of a big event (especially one with so little lead time, which challenged her significant special event planning skills), but she did ask Donte one thing: "ensure you deliver Rolando and Ernesto to the orphanage dining hall no later than 6:15. PLEASE! The event will start at 6:30 sharp," she reminded him, "and several stations plan to cut in at 6:40 for Stoyonovich's brief remarks and check presentation to the Orphanage Executive Director."

"Will do. See you soon!" Donte signed off.

Less than a minute later came her reply from her Droid: "looking 4ward to it!"

* * *

Gnawing at Donte during this preparatory period was the uncertainty he felt toward Ronko Stoyonovich, the key player in all this. First, was the outburst by Stoyonovich at Senator Dawson's party. Next, when he and Grace were making the presentation at his firm's headquarters, Donte saw firsthand the mercurial mood swing of the Czech émigré upon being challenged about the logo design. Finally, there was the Stoyonix Company's complete capitulation to all the terms, resulting in the Saint Celestin presentation-fundraising event. Something wasn't adding up, so Donte decided to do a cursory Internet investigation, with the few hours remaining before the evening's festivities.

For an online megastar, little had been written about Ronko Stoyonovich, at least that shed insight into his complex personality. Donte found the standard fare that detailed "Stoyo's" meteoric rise to the semi-top in the semi-conductor world, culminating with a major settlement package from Google, where he was one of the original players. His "retirement" appeared to come under a cloud of suspicion that one report referred to as *i-spionage*. In fact, this particular computer magazine headline read "I Spi" and detailed how Ronko and his future partner were accused of stealing secrets from a rival company in Silicon Valley and purportedly tried to persuade Google to incorporate the new technology. He was politely "let go" and paid a very handsome severance package. But due to a three-year non-compete agreement, Stoyonovich was forced to the high-tech sidelines in the early part of the new millennium. It couldn't have come at a more perfect time. Due to a gift from the gods, Stoyonovich got out with his millions at the exact moment the "dot-com bubble" burst. While mega-millionaires watched their fortunes vanish into the ether just as quickly as they had been created, Stoyonovich quietly went underground. Over the next three years he developed an idea for a new company that revolved around the concept of "cloud computing."

Donte didn't have a clue what "cloud computing" referred to, but he quickly found out with some Internet research. According to the National Institute of Standards and Technology website:

Cloud computing is a model for enabling convenient, on-demand network access to a shared pool of configurable computing resources (e.g., networks, servers, storage, applications, and services) that can be rapidly provisioned and released with minimal management effort or service provider interaction.

He learned that the key characteristics of cloud computing were on-demand self-service, broad network access, resource pooling, rapid elasticity, and measured service. In five short years following the start of his company, Stoyonix had catapulted to the top of cloud computing, a service still in its infancy but offering unimaginable riches for those with the vision.

One final news report provided a hint at the Stoyo personality Donte was seeking. A small, up-and-coming southern California firm specializing in online holiday boutique items had filed a lawsuit against Stoyonix less than a year ago. The company charged that Stoyonix failed to deliver adequate server space during the crucial

Christmas holiday selling season, causing immeasurable losses. The suit claimed that at the same time that the Stoyonix servers had supposedly "crashed," Ronko was preparing to fund the launch of a rival holiday gift company, one owned by his brother-in-law, which effectively abridged the terms of agreement. The two parties settled out of court, but the exchange left a stain on Stoyonovich's reputation, and provided insight into the man running the company, mused Donte. The article reminded him of something Grandfather Antonio often told him: "A man's word is his bond. And his reputation is all that remains after he leaves this Earth."

* * *

Around 2:30 that afternoon, Grace felt her Droid vibrating with an incoming text message. It was from Donte, warning her that he had "a bad feeling that Ronko Stoyonovich is going to pull a sneaky fast one on us tonight. Do we have alternatives?"

Grace glared at the Droid and entertained thoughts of hurling the device across the orphanage Great Hall, where staffers from her firm were knee deep in boughs of evergreens and crimson bows scattered across the floor. Grace texted back a simple response, one she was sure Donte would understand: "have faith—believe."

Donte grimaced at the response. He should have had better sense than to bother Graciella so near deadline. He checked the clock: just over four hours to do three herculean tasks, one which must be completed at the workshop. He phoned Jamas and asked him to handle the last job—and meet them at the orphanage by 6:30.

CHAPTER EIGHT

When Donte led his father and uncle inside Saint Celestin Orphanage, the dining hall had been converted to a winter wonderland. They were surrounded by forests of freshly cut evergreen trees, dozens of wreaths and hundreds and hundreds of twinkling bulbs providing soft, inspiring illumination throughout the hall. A female staffer from Capital Communications approached them wearing a forest green sweater with her company's logo embroidered in white. She escorted the Solteros toward the front of the hall, where a wooden riser, carpeted in crimson, and ringed with poinsettia plants, would serve as the presentation platform. Lined up on a small table sitting at the lip of the riser was a dozen Soltero Christmas Wish Holders. Behind the table was a microphone and PA speakers mounted atop the portable stands. The young woman asked the Solteros to stay in the area, while other staffers were rounding up the Stoyonix group and Mrs. Anderson, the orphanage's Executive Director. The only thing missing from this Christmas postcard was the snow.

When Grace met the Stoyonix contingent in the parking lot she greeted the CEO with a firm handshake, and was introduced to Mr. Rigl, Legal Counsel, and her counterpart, Sheila Malvory, Communications VP. "Lead the way," Stoyonovich said confidently.

Grace stopped to glance behind them. "Um, did you remember the check?" Stoyonovich appeared confused, responding with a half-witted, non-plused expression.

"The oversized check for the Stoyonix donation to kick-start the fundraiser tonight."

Stoyonovich reached behind Grace with his left arm, gently nudging her to lead the way, but she wouldn't budge. "I'm afraid there's been some miscommunication between our two staffs, Ms. McBride."

"What sort of miscommunication?" Grace raised her voice. Minutes before a major event she grew tense when a loose end of this size became unraveled. "We had an agreement."

"You see, Grace, I never agreed to such a thing," Stoyonovich said, jabbing his three button holiday red vest. "And I'm afraid Sheila here misconstrued my desire to help you raise some money. But I never agreed for Stoyonix to contribute any cash."

"But that's the cornerstone of our drive that starts," she said checking her watch, "in less than fifteen minutes."

Stoyonovich tossed up his hands. "Never sweat the small stuff, Ms. McBride. Now, shall we go inside and raise some money for these little monkeys? It's cold out here."

Grace came to a firm halt. "Mr. Stoyonovich—we had a deal. And I've got it in writing."

"Listen, I don't know what went on between you and Sheila, but you should be happy we even made it to this little soiree. Hell, it's snowin' so damn hard in Nevada City we barely made it down the mountain." The ring of a cell phone interrupted their conversation. Sheila answered, and held it out for Stoyonovich.

"Governor's chief of staff—just wanted to make sure we'll be there as planned." Stoyonovich took the phone.

"Hello, Margo. Yes, dear. We're in Sacramento now. We've just got this little event here at the orphanage, and we should be there by. . . 7:30 tops." Stoyonovich smiled down at the wet asphalt. "You just wanted to know whether to release my seat at the governor's table. No, that seat will be occupied, Margo dear, by me, yes." Stoyonovich laughed, clicked off the phone and handed it back to his Communications VP. He looked around. "Where's McBride?"

Bernard Rigl pointed in the direction of the Great Hall. Grace was some thirty yards in the lead and steaming toward the entrance.

"I guess that's the way," Stoyonovich said with a chuckle, walking with his group. "I've noticed that tall broads tend to get huffy too easily in times of stress," he said, placing his arm around the waist of his Communications chief. "Of course, Sheila, you're the exception."

* * *

Inside the Great Hall of the orphanage stood a gaggle of young children, dressed in white gowns, legs shuffling, arms bouncing and necks twitching, as they awaited their big moment on television.

Television camera crews had set up their positions in back of the hall, with their imposing lights shining brightly next to the high-def cameras mounted atop the tripods that supported them. Reporters were scrambling throughout the hall, gathering information for their pre-interview segments. Donte found himself in one such interview with the reporter from TV37, an independent channel, asking him to explain the hidden meaning of the Wish Holder design.

As he had just begun addressing the interviewer's question, Graciella walked toward him in overdrive. She moved behind the camera and without saying a word gave the universal "cut" signal across her throat and mouthed the word "now" with a short head bob to indicate the general direction: the corner area nearest the stage.

Donte finished his statement and excused himself. He found Grace pivoting on her high heels, waiting for him. Before he could ask "what the hell?" she broke in. "You were right."

"About. . . ?"

"The guy's a snake in the grass," she said, clicking her right heel on the linoleum. "Bastard."

"What's wrong? Tell me," he urged Grace.

"They've backed out of the fundraiser. Didn't bring the check. No donation."

Donte reached out and grabbed her forearm. "Easy. Easy. Are they still going to participate here in the fundraiser at all?" She nodded, unable to speak she was so angry. "I guess that means it was a good thing, then, that I made up this board here," he said, reaching for a foam core poster leaning against the wall, ". . . with the web address of our donation site printed on it."

Grace appeared confused and excited in one fluid expression. "Web site?"

"Yes, the one I created today so that our viewers can donate to the fundraiser." He held up the board.

Saint Celestin Orphanage Fundraiser
SaintCelestinFunds.org
Donations welcome. All credit cards accepted

"*Ohmygod*, you're brilliant! You knew all along, you tried to warn me. . . " She saw the Stoyonix group approaching and became incensed at the site of the snarky Stoyonovich. She hoped Donte would hold her back if she gave in to her instincts and punched the little bastard in that smarmy smile of his.

Donte grabbed her by the shoulders. "Listen. You've had a lot to do to put on this event. I just provided a little backup, that's all."

"And now it looks like—*maybe*—we can pull this thing off."

"We can, but I need one more big favor," he said, holding his index finger directly in front of his face. "I need you to slightly rearrange the schedule."

* * *

The next few minutes flew by and came to a sudden halt when the principals were invited onstage. Rolando followed Ernesto, who followed Donte up on the riser. Ronko Stoyonovich was already standing up there near the mike. Grace signaled to Mrs. Anderson to bring the children in front of the riser, where she was assisted by a Capital Communications staffer in arranging the children in a perfect semi-circle.

"If I could have everyone's attention," Grace McBride said, her voice echoing throughout the hall. "We have some excited young visitors here," she said, gesturing to the twelve angelically-dressed children standing before the platform. "They have been on their very best behavior." She paused, as more people entering the hall quietly came to attention. She had waited until you could hear a reporter's pen drop on the floor. "We should begin."

With the skill of a United Nations representative, and showing none of the anger she displayed just seven minutes ago, Grace succinctly summarized the events that led to this night. With elegant and cogently worded statements, she explained that two business entities, from opposite positions in the marketplace, had reconciled their differences and elected to unite this evening to benefit the children of the Saint Celestin Orphanage. The crowd applauded at the appropriate moment, as Grace looked around the room, making eye contact with all key segments, including the building janitor far off in the back of the hall, bewildered by the bright lights and fanfare.

"At this time, it is my privilege to introduce the founder and president of Stoyonix Corporation, Mister Ronko Stoyonovich."

Squinting in the glare on the camera lights, Stoyonovich stared off toward the back of the hall like a congressional politician standing out on the Capitol steps. He appeared alert, confident and clearly enjoying the attention. And being a shrewd and successful businessman, he knew he had a few short minutes to accomplish several things. So, he kept his remarks succinct. He thanked the Soltero family for their contribution of the Wish Holders, thanked Grace McBride for making this event possible, and then backed away from the microphone, turned to Grace with upturned palms and said, "I think it's time to kick off the fundraiser, right?"

Grace signaled for Donte to join them. He reached behind the stage, found the poster board and approached them at the microphone. Stoyonovich saw the oversized poster and immediately surmised the organizers had perpetrated a sneak attack.

"Hey, what's the deal here. . . " he said, checking the back side of the poster. He assumed it included the check committing his company to the $5,000 donation they had originally agreed to. When he saw the backside was blank, he realized he had jumped the gun, and quickly reassumed his nonchalant demeanor.

While cameras closed in on the company president, he explained that Stoyonix was appealing to all those watching throughout the Sacramento Valley and the foothills, "to join me in making cash donations to the orphanage. In the next few days leading up to Christmas, we ask the viewers out there to match, eh, er. . . to help us raise funds for the Saint Celestin Orphanage, a very worthy cause, especially during this holiday season." He turned to Grace, who was holding one corner of the poster board, while Donte held the other side. "This our web site, here?" he asked, pointing to the web address. She confirmed with a nod.

". . . and so I challenge everyone watching tonight, to make their pledge on our web site, SaintCelestinFunds.org."

More applause in the hall, but before Stoyonovich had uttered "dot org," Grace had resumed control of the microphone. She had less than four minutes before the live television window would go dark. "Terrific. Thanks so much." Grace repeated the web address once more.

"Now, for the event you've all been waiting for—the presentation of the Christmas Wish Holders. But first," Grace turned behind her and gestured for the Solteros to step out front of the platform, which was Donte's cue to fetch the item his cousin Jamas had prepared at the workshop. Jamas brought it to him, with the scarf already opened.

"You know that it wasn't baked?" Jamas reminded him.

Donte nodded, taking the object from his cousin. "Understood. And you were generous with the dust?"

"Practically emptied the whole damn pouch." Jamas laughed aloud, then covered his mouth.

Donte winked, indicating his appreciation. He turned and headed for the mike to stand beside Grace.

"First, Donte Soltero would like to make a special presentation to Mr. Stoyonovich." A smile formed on the face of Ronk Stoyonovich, who obviously enjoyed the limelight. And he was a big fan of surprise moments. Donte approached with the Christmas Wish Holder in his hands. Carefully holding the object with one hand under the bottom, and the other firmly clasped atop the lid, Donte held it high for all to see, then said into the microphone ". . . for those at home, this is one of the *original* prototype Soltero Christmas Wish Holders. And this one was made personally for Mr. Stoyonovich."

This was not the surprise Stoyonovich had expected or hoped for. He accepted the object in the palms of his hands and examined it while running his fingers along the fluid "S" design on the front. "Feels a little tacky, a little wet still," Ronko said off-mic with a curious expression.

"Yeah, that's the special rainforest mist that makes it so unique." Donte rubbed his fingers together, simulating some undefined ethereal quality.

Ronko sensed sarcasm in the younger Soltero's voice, while trying to wipe the sticky residue from his fingers to his palm and eventually to the back of his hands. It wasn't coming off, and he was being rushed by Grace McBride, who indicated they needed to move along. She gestured for them to go down in front of the stage, quickly. Stoyonovich laid the Wish Holder back in the silken scarf Jamas had left on the riser and stepped down to join the others.

"At this time, we will make the presentation of the Soltero Christmas Wish Holders to the children of the orphanage." She and Donte passed out Holders to the older Soltero men, Mrs. Anderson of the orphanage, and the Stoyonix CEO. She instructed them to present one of the Rosewood boxes to each of the children. By this time, the children's semi-circle had morphed into a serpentine line, but it hardly mattered as the cameras happily zoomed in on the happy shining faces of the children gazing in wonder at the beautiful Holders they'd been handed as early Christmas presents. "All of the children here at Saint Celestin Orphanage will receive one of these Soltero Christmas Wish Holders," McBride told the audience, "and they are encouraged to write their wish on the cards tonight, in hopes that their wishes—which are supposed to benefit someone other than themselves—will be granted in time for Christmas."

* * *

Once Grace had spoken the word "Christmas" it provided a signal that the ceremony officially had ended. Chaos ensued, the kind that a twenty-three-year PR pro loves to see, as reporters from the local newspapers, blogs, radio and television stations sought out their guest interviews. The cameraman from Channel 13, the most aggressive station in community relations, had already removed his camera from the tripod, and was closing in on the beaming face of an African American girl, proudly holding up her Wish Holder. The cameraman slowly panned from her face to the card attached and zoomed in on the Stoyonix logo. At one point, Ronk Stoyonovich, Ernesto Soltero and Clare Anderson of the orphanage stood less than five feet apart, with cameras and microphones in their faces, addressing the disparate media in front of them. Even some of the children were being interviewed simultaneously.

Graciella grabbed Donte and rushed him off to an unoccupied corner away from the lights. "I need to talk with you about something." She sounded rushed. "It's important."

Donte smiled. "First off, congratulations. You did a marvelous job here tonight."

Grace gave a quick, dismissive wave. She had urgent business, and collecting kudos could wait until they had taken down the evergreen bunting. "Turns out I was way off in my estimation of the number of kids they house here at the orphanage," she told him. "Not nearly the 500 like I thought. More like 300 kids. But Mrs.

Anderson, bless her heart, has a solution. But I need your okay first."

"What is it?"

"She suggested we give the remaining Holders to the kids at the Sacramento Children's Home. Together, they have a joint operating agreement, so in effect it's all one big happy family. Now that still only makes 437 Holders distributed total, so we'll still have like sixty something left over."

"Okay, Ella. But what's the big deal?" Donte wondered. Out of the corner of his eye, he was watching one of the Stoyonix executives, the older man, who was standing only a few feet away, appearing to listen in on their conversation. "We were prepared to give away the entire 500."

"That's just it," Grace said. "We committed to Stoyonix that we wouldn't sell any of the Holders. We—*you*—can't profit from them, so we need to give them all away to comply with the terms of the agreement."

The older Stoyonix executive moved closer and squeezed between them. "Excuse me, Ms. McBride" he said, placing his arms around both of them, "but I couldn't help but overhear you." He grinned. "Actually, I was eavesdropping."

The man introduced himself: Bernard Rigl, Stoyonix Legal Counsel. "I wouldn't worry about those conditions you were alluding to, Ms. McBride," he said. "Hell, I'm the one who forced them on you in the first place." His broad smile assured them this would not present a problem.

"Thank goodness," Grace gave a sigh of relief. "Now, if you don't mind, I'm needed by one of the TV crews. Can you two work this out?"

"Certainly, go on," Rigl told her. Turning back to Donte, he said, "Mister Soltero..."

"Donte..."

"Donte, I have a solution to the problem Ms. McBride just described. If you, your father and your uncle will allow me, I would like to take possession of fifty of those remaining Wish Holders. We have a small children's home of our own in Nevada City, and I would love to give them as presents to the children there. Would you be amenable to that?" Donte couldn't see any reason why he shouldn't, as he had just explained to Grace, the Solteros had expected that all the Holders would be given away. But before he could respond, Rigl pulled out his checkbook and Mont Blanc pen from his jacket, and began writing a check. He ripped it from the checkbook and handed it to Donte.

"Ten thousand dollars. Mr. Rigl, I'm afraid you've overpaid here, by..." Donte started to work the math in his head, when Rigl interrupted him.

"Four times, I know." Placing the checkbook and pen back in his jacket, Rigl said, "Do you know why?"

The younger man looked around the room and then directly into the attorney's eyes. "Perhaps because your daughter, who was dying last week in the Oncology Ward at the Med Center, was just found to be cancer free?" Donte watched the smile on Rigl's face turn to astonishment. "And you think that our Christmas Wish Holder may have contributed to her recovery."

"I won't ask how you know that," the older man said. Patting Donte on the arm, he added, "But I would gladly pay ten times that amount, Mister Soltero. For you see, you have helped to make this the most glorious Christmas of my life."

Watching from a few feet away, Uncle Rollie patiently waited until their conversation appeared to have ended, then walked up to his nephew. He arrived just as Donte turned to ask the attorney one final question. "Wait, Mr. Rigl. That still leaves thirteen."

The attorney turned and grinned. "Hell, they're yours. Take 'em."

Uncle Rolando nodded. "Good. And I'm taking one of them right now on my way home."

"Where you going, Uncle Rollie?"

"To the LeValier house," he said, waving off his nephew. "That lady paid nearly as much as that crazy attorney. In fact, I may as well take that one over there on the stage," he said.

Donte suddenly felt exhausted; he had accomplished much in so little time. Maybe now he could head for home, he thought, while watching his uncle ambling across the floor. When Rolando had reached the riser and started to bend down to pick up the Wish Holder lying in the scarf, it suddenly hit him. "Wait! Uncle Rollie, don't touch it." Donte ran over just in time. "Not that one."

Rollie turned around. "Why not?"

"Well, that's the one we gave to Mr. Stoyonovich."

"Yes, but he left it here." The uncle pointed to the object. "Seems he does not want it." Both men checked around the room. Apparently, the Stoyonix CEO had already left.

"Eh, well, I'm gonna ship it to him," Donte said, wrapping the scarf around the wooden object. He carefully picked it up and cradled it in the crook of his arm.

The uncle noticed Donte acting suspiciously. "Oh, I see. That's the one you asked Jamas to prepare with the *extra* pinch of that fairy dust, eh?" The old man grinned a knowing smile. "Alright. I'll pick up another one at the studio tomorrow."

A reporter for Channel 10 had been hanging off to the side waiting for the younger Soltero to finish the personal conversations. She moved in and asked for an interview. As her cameraman adjusted his equipment, she said "Did I overhear correctly: you have some of those Wish Holders left over?"

"Uh, yes, but. . . "

". . . because I would love to buy one for my Shannon. She would absolutely adore it."

"Well, they're all spoken for, I'm afraid," Donte said, knowing it was just a white lie.

The reporter rolled her microphone, as if to say, "Well—I tried," and then signaled to her photographer to turn on the camera lights, as she proceeded to interview Donte Soltero.

CHAPTER NINE

Later that evening, when Donte arrived home, Alena greeted him inside the foyer. "Hungry?" When he admitted he was starving, she led him in the family room and asked Anthony, who was sitting on the couch, to give her the remote. At first he objected, and when she explained she wanted to show her father the recording of the evening's festivities, he flipped the remote in the air with his left hand and went into the kitchen.

Alena fired up the DVR and cued it to the Channel 13 coverage of the Christmas Wish Holder dedication. "You sit," she said to her father, "and I'll get you some leftovers." She was clearly jazzed about the event's outcome and wanted to share it with her father, and get his reaction to what he had seen in person.

As Donte began to watch the television replay, he was suddenly distracted by Alena yelling at her brother. She had caught Anthony eating the last of the rewarmed spaghetti she had been saving for her father.

"Hey, no yelling!" Donte yelled into the kitchen. "It's okay, I'm not that hungry."

Alena opened the refrigerator, grabbed a beer and sat down with her father on the couch. She tossed a bag of chips next to him and cracked open the beer bottle. "Here." Alena took control of the remote. While they watched the camera zoom in on Grace McBride's face during her opening remarks Alena marveled, "She's unbelievable."

"She's good," Donte admitted. "She's very good."

"Watch this, Dad," the girl said pointing to when Graciella introduced Rolando, Ernesto and then Donte Soltero. "See the way she looked at you?"

Donte shook his head. "No, what do you mean."

"Look!" Alena's voice rose. "She's got the hots for you, Dad."

"What?" Donte thought his daughter might have been drinking before he had arrived home. "Get outta here."

"Muy caliente. Seriously," the girl said, rewinding the DVR to the place where Grace smiled as she introduced Donte. "You can see it her eyes. Look, they're sparkling. That woman has the hots for you."

Anthony's bowl clattered in the sink, obviously disgusted at the notion of post-thirty-something sex. "I'm outta here."

Donte turned back to the kitchen. "Where you goin'?" His son didn't bother to answer as he continued down the hallway to the den room.

Alena allowed the television coverage to continue playing, sitting with her arms crossed and the remote tucked between her legs. "Seriously, this woman is a media god." She shook her head and corrected herself. "Goddess."

"She's very, very good," Donte allowed a second time.

Alena faced her father. "Are you telling me you

don't feel anything for Graciella?"

He stared at her as if a fellow light rail passenger had asked if Donte knew his shoe was untied. "Yes. We're friends. Good friends. That's all." He ate a mouthful of chips and washed it down with beer. "Friends."

"Well, I am telling you that this woman has the hots for you, and you are crazy to sit on this couch and not ask her out."

Donte sat upright, scattering potato chips from the bag onto the carpet. "What do you want me to do? Tell me."

"Go after her! She obviously wants you. I could see it the other night here at dinner."

"Listen," Donte said, trying to reassert himself, "that woman is out of my league. Do you understand? O-U-T, out of my league. She's schmoozing with guys like Ronko Stoyonovich here, Mr. Billion bucks, and the governor of California every other week, for cryin' out loud. You think she wants some old retread high school boyfriend? And a second-level designer to boot, huh?"

"Wow, Dad," her voice lowered to a calm pitch. "You really have a problem. But all I can tell you is what I see, and I see a very attractive, successful woman," the girl stabbed at the screen for punctuated effect, "who looks at you with a sparkle in her eye. And, if I was you, a middle-aged widower, and a woman like that looked at me, I'd be white on rice all over it." Alena got up from the couch, accidentally crunching chips in the carpet. She stopped and turned toward her father. "I'm just sayin'." Then she left the room.

"Well, I'm just sayin'," he called toward Alena who was storming down the hallway. "Your mother's been gone less than a year, and you got me frothin' over some PR queen bee, just because. . . " Her bedroom door slammed behind her. ". . . you think there's a sparkle in her eye!

"Sparkle, my ass," he yelled. Donte turned back to watching the television replay of the children receiving the Christmas Wish Holders. "She is very good, I'll give her that."

* * *

Donte flipped over to live television and watched the end of a college basketball game. When the game was over, he switched to the local FOX channel to check out the 10 o'clock news. The opening teaser naturally was about the weather, and how the snowline had fallen down below the 700-foot level. The telecast continued: ". . . and if you think our weather is crazy, wait 'til you see what a top Internet guru said at the governor's banquet tonight!" Donte sat upright and grabbed the remote. He wondered if this could possibly be related to Stoyonovich. *Who else could it be?* He didn't have to wait long, as the newscast soon cut over to a live report at the Sutter Club where Governor Timmerman held her first annual governor's banquet. The report began:

". . . numerous Hollywood celebrities, titans of industry and local officials were feted by Governor Timmerman and came away highly entertained this evening—and that was *before* the comedy duo Jeffers'n'Simmons came on. During an acceptance speech by Stoyonix CEO Ronko Stoyonovich, who was there to pick up 'Entrepreneur of the Year' award, things turned extremely strange. Stoyonovich obviously had been imbibing in something stronger than the champagne served that evening," the reporter detailed. Then he played highlights of Ronko's speech which included: *rumors that I stole secrets from SynchTronics are true—all true*; *I once killed a Russian captain for calling me stupid to my face;* and finally *all these little black creatures are coming to attack me!*

"Truly weird," said the reporter, shaking his head and smiling in disbelief.

"Perhaps it's due to oxygen deprivation," he quipped, "from having been up in the 'clouds' too long." An obvious tongue-in-cheek reference to Stoyonix' cloud computing business activities. Donte shut off the television, stupefied. His plan for "punking" the egotistical businessman had gone way beyond his expectations.

* * *

The next morning, Donte immediately flipped on the television and saw where the CEO's remarks were carried by all the business press. As a result, by midmorning Stoyonix stock price had dropped 13 percent. *Whew. . . way too much shaman's dust*, he thought of the heavy dose he instructed Jamas to apply to the face of the Wish Holder yesterday. Moreover, Jamas didn't have time to "bake" the final product, sealing the paint, dust and varnish, which accounted for the fresh, 'tacky' feel. He then realized that the chemical reaction undoubtedly had entered Stoyonovich's bloodstream on a delayed basis and didn't take effect until ninety minutes later, when the CEO stood at the podium to accept his award, and displayed his true colors. Donte swore he would never do it again—at least, not like that. *Maybe there really is something to that shaman's spell*, he mused.

On the positive side, when he signed online to the new Saint Celestin web site he had set up, he was absolutely astounded: 437 individuals had made donations of the recommended amount of $25, resulting in contributions totaling $10,925. In less than twenty-four hours, they'd collected nearly as much as Stoyonix had promised to help raise for the orphanage.

He immediately sent Grace a congratulatory email on the event, and in the middle of the message repeated Alena's compliment she was a "media goddess." He also hinted that the online donations received so far were exceeding his hopes, but did not reveal the total collection. He figured he'd wait until it was settled and the tabulations "official."

Grace quickly replied with a text message, thanking him for his good work and heads up fallback planning. "Too bad didn't have more time," she added. "Would have est. a mobile donor site 2. Just text 'SAINT' or the like. But glad U thought of web site!"

She concluded with a final jab at the Stoyonix CEO: "Stoyo is a snake! And a drunk. Got what he dezvrd last night."

Although he wanted to pick up the phone and chat with Grace more about their successful event, he knew she would be completely exhausted. Besides, a little distance was probably a good thing at this point, despite what Alena said last night.

Meanwhile, he had plenty to do with last minute holiday errands, including finishing shopping for the kids. He invited Alena to join him at the downtown mall, but she turned him down, saying "That place sucks." He offered to take her to Arden Fair, a traditional two-tier, enclosed shopping experience, but she wasn't interested. When he agreed to drive all the way out to the Roseville Galleria, the largest and newest shopping mall in the greater Sacramento area, where they could have lunch and then shop, and she still declined, he realized it was a lost cause. Alena remained miffed that her father wouldn't listen to her feminine advice, and she was driving the point home with the best teenaged tactics available to her.

* * *

In addition to completing his Christmas shopping, Donte spent the better part of one afternoon buying the turkey and holiday trimmings at the grocery store for their annual family Christmas feast. He picked out a fifteen-pound bird that would leave lots of leftovers. When he exited the store, the shopping basket was overflowing. More importantly, he was hoping Alena would thaw out by then, as he was counting on her sage advice when it came to cooking the turkey and stuffing, knowing that she had paid much closer attention to Maria's cooking skills than he had ever had.

In between gift and grocery shopping, he also went out to lunch with an old friend who said he might have a lead on some graphic design work. Admittedly, Donte felt anxious about his future prospects, as he had allowed his graphic design business to lapse while he concentrated on the Christmas Wish Holder project. In retrospect, this project had required far more time than he had ever expected. Fortunately, that cash donation from attorney Rigl would go a long way to offset the expenses incurred in designing, fabricating and decorating the holiday Wish Holders.

He called his father and asked if he planned to be at the workshop tomorrow? "I figured we could settle up on this project. I'll bring over the expense receipts and cash." Ernesto reminded him that it was Christmas Eve, and Rolando would be out of town visiting his wife's relatives, but he figured it wouldn't be a problem.

"You bring the coffee," the father said.

CHAPTER TEN

Donte left the house early on Christmas Eve. He started off the morning by visiting Saint Mary's Cemetery, where he placed flowers on the graves of Maria and his mother Eva, and said a brief prayer for each of them. He dutifully made the rounds, visiting Ernesto's parents, as well his maternal grandparents' gravesites. All of them had been interned in the walls there at the cemetery. Only Maria requested to be buried in the ground; an old fashioned traditionalist to the end, Donte mused.

Staring at the crypt of his grandmother Alaina Carvalho, he was immediately whisked to the kitchen of her home at the 400 block of "S" Street, and could see her opening the oven door, and pulling out the loaves of *biscoitos* or Portuguese sweet bread she was baking for her grandchildren.

As the ethereal image of his grandmother dissipated, he remained in the moment, remembering the warm and toasty environment of her kitchen and the wonderful smells emanating from the eggs, milk, flour, sugar, salt, cinnamon, and nutmeg that had been combined in this miraculous creation that the women baked and served each Christmas morning. And just as quickly as he had resurrected this romanticized moment from his childhood, he snapped back to the cold hard reality of the present. Standing on the icy concrete in front of his grandmother's crypt, Donte Soltero began to ache inside, not because he would never see his grandmother again, for she had died decades ago, but because he realized that, with his wife now gone, this would be the first year there would be no one to bake and serve him a loaf of Portuguese sweet bread as Grandma Alaina, his mother Eva, and wife Maria had done for him every Christmas morning of his life.

After leaving the cemetery Donte drove over to Peet's Coffee and picked up a couple of drinks and a goodie for his father, knowing he would be expecting it after the last time Grace hosted an event in the conference room. When he walked in the workshop, he found his father inside reading the morning paper while enjoying the solitude of the conference room.

"'Bout time you got here," said Ernie. "I need my morning coffee." The son placed the coffee in front of his father and sat across from him at the table without saying a word. "You visit the cemetery this morning?"

Donte nodded, blowing steam from the lid on the coffee cup.

"I can always tell," said Ernesto.

* * *

Alena had gotten up late that morning, and when she shuffled into the kitchen in her extra-long T-shirt overhanging the navy blue sweatpants, the house was dark. She knew her father had already been up and gone when she found the newspaper on the kitchen table. She checked the coffee carafe, but there was none left. Too sleepy to bother making coffee herself, she filled the tea kettle and set it over the gas flame. The front page of the paper reminded her that it was Christmas Eve and probably time she started speaking again to her father. She felt guilty, wondering if she had been too harsh in giving him the silent treatment over their squabble the other night.

When the kettle reached a boil, she pulled down a ceramic mug from the cabinet and poured the water into the cup. The phone rang, jarring her contemplative quiet mood. Silently, she hoped it was her father so she could begin letting him into her good graces.

"Good morning, Alena." Grace McBride was calling.

"Hey," Alena said sleepily, slipping the tea bag into the steaming hot water.

"Merry Christmas Eve," the older woman said, stretching the final word into a nauseating sing-songy treatment.

"You, too," Alena sang obligingly. It was still too early for idle palaver, even if it was the 'media goddess.' "What's up?"

"Well, I was trying to reach your father. Is he home?"

Alena explained that he'd gone out early, and she should try his cell phone. Graciella countered that she had done that, but there was no answer. "Well, he could be anywhere, then. I dunno. We really haven't talked much since your big Christmas pageant." Alena scrunched her eyes and hunched her shoulders at the faux pax; it was just too early for adult conversation, especially this particular one.

"Why, what happened?"

"Well, we got into this argument," Alena began, "and it sorta was about you and him."

Graciella chuckled. "Argument over me and your father. I don't understand."

Alena started to sip her tea, but the cup was scalding to the touch. She laid it back down on the tile. "Oh, you know, adult-type stuff."

Graciella could sense that Alena was not in the best of moods, nor was she in a position to want to divulge details. "Okay, well if he comes in, will you ask him to call me? It's kind of important. And I've got some really great news. . . "

"Really, what a surprise." This time she knew her sarcasm had crossed way over the line.

Having handled difficult employee situations many times in the past, Grace could sense when a disgruntled young woman was grappling with a problem. "Is there something I should know? Did I do something to upset your dad? Or you, maybe?" Graciella appeared so sweet and vulnerable, and that appealed to Alena every time.

"Well, I was showing my dad the TV coverage of your event, you know, I had DVR'd it, and I just commented that it seemed obvious to me that you really liked him. And we got into this big argument about whether you do like him or if it's just my imagination. And I thought I had video evidence!" Alena smacked her palm on the kitchen tile, the reverberation stinging through the phone line. "And he wouldn't listen. So when I tried to prove my point he just told me to mind my own business, because I'm just, you know, a stupid teenager, and then he admitted to what the problem is."

Grace wasn't sure if this pause was her cue to cut in or Alena preparing to slap the tile again. "And what was that?"

"That he's intimidated by you. You know, you're drop-dead gorgeous, got a great figure for an older babe, and you're like this media goddess who meets with business tycoons and the governor, and he just thinks he's out of your league. Yeah. . . intimidated."

Grace waited a moment before quietly admitting, "Well, you're right."

"Yeah. Right about what?"

"That I like him."

"No, I meant like in a couple-ish kind of way."

"No, you're right, I'm attracted to your father. Always have been." Grace realized that last comment could be misconstrued, so she amended it quickly. "From a safe distance, yes, I've always been attracted to him."

"Well, you've got to tell him, then. . . " Alena felt awake now, and wanted to throw the conversation in to high gear.

"'Lena? 'Lena, hold on, I have. I've been trying these past two weeks. He's not ready."

"What are you talking about?"

"He's not ready for someone new in his life. At least, not me." Grace paused for effect. "He still cares for your mother, it's perfectly natural. He needs time. And you can't push him into a new relationship until he's ready."

Alena began to cry, silently. "Yeah, but you're perfect for him, Grace."

"Doesn't matter, darlin'," she said, borrowing Ernesto's affectionate term that she knew would resonate with the young woman.

"I just don't want my dad to lose a good thing and be all alone the rest of his life." Alena sniffled. "I'm just sayin'."

"Alena, you couldn't have said it more beautifully. Now, I've got to go, okay. Got a lot to do today."

"Grace," Alena said. "Are you going to come to midnight mass at the cathedral tonight?"

The question took her completely by surprise. "I dunno. Hadn't even thought of it. Your father hadn't mentioned it, certainly, so I didn't know it was something you guys did." Alena's sniffles could be heard again. "Remember. . . when *he's* ready."

"Okay," Alena quickly brightened. "If I don't see you, have a Merry Christmas."

"You, too, 'Lena."

* * *

Donte had propped his feet up on the conference table, while blowing smoke rings from his "victory" cigar. He had run through all his receipts from the Christmas Wish Holder project and came out ahead $187. That he could gloat and smoke at the same time amazed his father. "You're a regular Rockefeller.

"Now would you take that disgusting thing outside?" his father groused. "You're smellin' up the place."

Dante shook his head, and blew out a sustained

stream of cigar smoke, just to irritate his father. "Too damn cold outside," he said. "Might snow later today, Dad."

"Cold. You don't know the first thing about cold," he groused some more. "Cold is when you wake up at 5:30 in the morning, the house so dark and frosty, you can see your breath in your bedroom. That's cold, mister." Ernesto shook his head, as his son sat there mocking him with a smile. "Eskimo cold."

Donte decided it was a good time to change the subject and mentioned that he had some ideas for the design of next year's Wish Holder. Ernest exhaled a dismissive *pfffftt*. He didn't want to hear about next year's project "until there's fruit on my tomato bushes."

"What are you sayin', Dad. You're not excited about another successful Soltero Brothers and Sons venture?" He pronounced it dramatically, mostly to be silly. But it had crossed his mind.

"Son, we're in the final year of a five-year lease. I don't know what the future holds."

Donte lowered his feet back on the floor, with a concerned look on his face. "What are you saying, Dad?"

"Who knows what's around bend, that's what I'm sayin'. You're uncle's getting along in years. . . "

"Aww, he's still spry," Donte countered.

"I know. But what age is he. . . ?" Ernest wondered, trying to do the math. He was 74, his brother, always three years older. "Goin' on pert near 78, son. Might not be able to do this much longer."

Donte sat quietly, contemplating a future he'd never considered. Not after all they had just gone through. The thought that the Soltero family business could end with a whimper—sooner than later—didn't sit well with him. After all, it was their business.

The tinkling of the bell on the front door snapped him from the reverie. "Hellooo," called a familiar, friendly female voice. "Merry Christmas. . . "

"We're in here," Ernesto yelled through the conference room doorway. He looked at his son with a furrowed brow. "Go on, go greet her," he whispered. But before Donte removed his boots from the table and rose from his chair, Graciella entered the room.

She was bundled warm in a white, mohair beret, taupe-colored winter coat and black lambskin gloves. Her cheeks were flushed pink from the cold, but her cocoa-colored eyes sparkled. "Have you heard the news!" she said excitedly.

"Yeah, it's nearly Christmas!" Ernesto laughed at his silly joke.

"Of course and a merry one it will be, too, for lots of people. Thanks to the Soltero Wish Holders."

"Why? What happened?" asked Donte.

"You'll never believe it. I just got a call from the Executive Director at the orphanage, Mrs. Anderson. She says three of the children have reported that their wishes have come true!"

"What?" Ernest appeared confused. He never imagined the wish part may actually work.

Grace went on to detail the three cases. "One of the children had wished his aunt would recover from a chronic hip condition. She did and was able to request that the child be placed in her custody. Another young girl, you remember the African American girl at the event, the one that was so cute, she'd wished that her younger brother would speak again. This boy hadn't spoken a word since they were placed there two years ago by the state. Then yesterday morning, suddenly he greeted his sister with 'Merry Christmas.'

"And the third one, oh, wait until you hear this. . . " Graciella told the story about a homeless family who this past fall had been living in a tent along the American River, "and when the police kicked them off the site, they went to pack up, but they couldn't find the nine-year-old girl. Searched everywhere for her, but no luck. Turns out, she'd been kidnapped by some vagabonds, who eventually dropped her off at the orphanage, unharmed. Lo and behold, the family eventually checked at the orphanage, and they found their little girl! Right after she'd entered her wish in the Holder.

"They are positively ecstatic over there!" Grace said, hugging Ernest. "It's a miracle."

"Yep, miracle on 34th Street," he quipped.

"Oh, *very* good," Grace said, impressed by the older man's word play.

Ernest gestured toward Donte. "My son. . . he may not be the brightest bulb in the pack, but you gotta say this for him—he's got heart." While putting on his winter muffler and overcoat, Ernie asked his son if he would be joining the grandkids for midnight mass? Donte shrugged. He was still unsure. Ernest gave Grace a quick peck on the cheek, waved goodbye and headed for the door. They heard the door close behind him and the tinkling of the bell.

Grace rose and fastened the top button on her coat, signaling she was preparing to leave. "Well, I just dropped by to share that great news. I knew you'd want to hear it."

Donte followed her out into the workshop. She noticed the twelve remaining Christmas Wish Holders, standing at attention inside the glass counter shelves. "Twelve," she mused. "Interesting number. Same number as the apostles. . . "

". . . or months in a year."

Not wishing to be outplayed, she added ". . . or signs in the Zodiac."

Donte paused at her sweet naiveté. "Same thing, darlin'." She grimaced with the face of a game show contestant who'd just heard the buzzer indicating an incorrect guess. He continued the game. "Your *age. . .* when I met you in middle school," Donte said alluringly. The teasing laugh that followed ensured she didn't misconstrue he was being overtly saccharine.

As she started to reach for the door handle, he asked her, "So, what're your plans for Christmas?"

"Well, tomorrow morning, I'll head out for San Rafael. My brother and his family always have a dinner." She nodded, balancing on the ball of her foot, waiting for the next move. *If* there would be a next move. *Perhaps an invitation to join the Soltero family at midnight mass*. She was actually looking forward to going now.

Instead, Donte held up his index finger to signal that she should wait one minute more. He walked across the workshop, reached into one of the wooden cubbies where Uncle Rolando stored the wood-working tools, and pulled out an object wrapped in a scarf. As he approached, she recognized the pattern was the same scarf they had used to cover the prototype Holder they delivered to Stoyonix Corporation that eventful morning. Carefully, and respectfully, Donte peeled away the layers of the colorful material, finally exposing a Christmas Wish Holder that easily was the prettiest she had seen. The veins running through the wood had created a gorgeous pattern all around. But it was the unique strokes that formed the "S" design that mesmerized her. She could tell that this was an early version of the logo, not quite as refined as those they had delivered to the orphanage. It was beautiful.

She looked up. "My very own Wish Holder," she said, with a curious lilt at the end. Then a pixie-like expression came over her face. "Please tell me this isn't the same one you gave to Stoyonovich the other night."

Donte assured her it was not; this one, he told her, had been created for someone very special. "Now tonight, be sure to make your wish, write it down, and secure it inside before you go to sleep."

She looked intensely at his wonderfully sensitive eyes. "Donnie. . . you know I don't believe in magic."

He backed away, surprised and disappointed. "After the stories you just told us about those orphan kids!"

Grace laid the scarf down on the glass counter. "Yes, it worked for them. But I've never been one for good luck. Anything I've ever gotten, I worked hard for, trust me. It doesn't matter how much I *wish* for something," she said, clutching the Holder tightly to her chest, "that isn't going to suddenly make it come true. At least not my wishes." She looked down at the beautiful Holder, then up again into his soothing brown eyes. She wished at that moment that Donte's heart would awaken to her true feelings for him.

"Well, give it a try," he said, regaining his composure at her disappointing reaction to the gift. "And have faith; you've got to *believe*."

CHAPTER ELEVEN

Graciella drove from the workshop back to her office. The roads had become extremely icy and the slate gray skies portended snow flurries by evening.

When she entered her office, she greeted two female account executives leisurely drinking hot cocoa and chatting in the waiting area. One of them wearing a red sweater vest saw that Grace was carrying an object wrapped in a colorful material under her arm. "Could it be that someone received her very own Wish Holder for Christmas?" Grace shot a playful schoolyard wince at the woman before proceeding down the hallway. The woman turned to her associate with a wide eyed grin. "Yep, she got one."

When she reached her desk, Grace laid the object on its backside and unfolded the flower-pattern scarf, revealing the Bolivian Rosewood Holder with the brilliant "S" design on front. She marveled again at the wonderfully rich color and unusual veins running throughout the sides of the wood. She placed the Holder upright on her desk and stared at it. It was stunningly beautiful and she would cherish it forever.

Grace grabbed the card and brought it closer to her eyes. It was then she knew in fact this was one of the original prototypes, as the card had printing on just one side:

Write Your Wish to Make Someone's Dream Come True
Drop this card inside. Close lid tight. And believe...

And believe, she thought. *Maybe some other time.*

She moved the Holder to the back of her desk near the clock and began signing the staff's holiday bonus checks. She looked up when she heard her administrative assistant entering the room.

"Going to have those by noon?"

Grace nodded with a weary but pleasant smile. "Tell me again why these bonus checks can't be processed by the automatic deposit system?" They both knew it was a rhetorical question.

"Still going to release everyone at noon?" the woman asked, looking at Grace hopefully.

"Yes, of course. They're not getting any work done anyway," Grace chuckled, pushing the stack of checks off her desk.

"Oh, thank you, Mrs. Scrooge," the assistant said in a faux Cockney accent. "Thank you on be'alf of all the crew." She gathered the checks and turned for the door. Suddenly, she reversed course and met her supervisor's eyes. "Grace, have a Merry Christmas."

"You, too."

* * *

At home, Graciella ate a late, quiet dinner and decided to retire early. She closed the lights, slipped into a pair of warm cotton pajamas and planned to curl up in bed with the posthumous Michael Crichton novel she had been putting off. But first she decided to have some warm cocoa to celebrate the evening. She put on her slippers and walked into the kitchen.

Grace poured the milk in the cup and stuck it in the microwave. While waiting for it to heat, she brought out the tin of cocoa and the sugar bowl. Another :35 read the microwave. Her glance fell on the Wish Holder, standing alone on the butterscotch-colored tile. When the bell sounded, she brought down the milk and stirred in some cocoa and sugar until they had dissolved. As she went to shut off the stove light, her eyes fell once more on the Christmas Wish Holder. She scooped it up and returned to her bedroom.

Grace placed the cup of cocoa on a coaster on her nightstand while holding the Wish Holder. She stared at the wooden object, and then with an efficient twist, pulled the card from the lid. She reached into the nightstand and found a writing pen, placed the card on top of the stand and wrote: **Love-Forever**. Contemplating the import of her next move, she debated whether that was enough. Remembering that the wish was supposed to benefit someone other than oneself, she decided the two words were insufficient, and she added a third: **Donte**. Grace dropped the card into the Wish Holder, closed her eyes for several seconds and *believed*. Fitting the lid on tight, she scrambled back in bed, grabbed her novel and began to read.

She had just flipped the first page, when the phone rang. Her heart leapt like a love-smitten teenager. She grabbed the telephone console on the nightstand.

"Graciella, this is Ernie."

"Merry Christmas, Ernesto."

"And to you too, darlin'. Listen, I don't know if I mentioned this earlier, but we're all planning to attend midnight mass at the Cathedral." Grace smiled to herself. *How could I forget?* "So, I don't know what your plans are, but we'd love really love for you to join us."

Graciella declined, saying she had already jumped into bed and planned to turn in early. "I'm driving early tomorrow to be with my brother for Christmas. But thank you for the offer. Very sweet."

"Well, I hope you'll reconsider and we might still see you," he said, before hanging up.

Grace found herself regretting she hadn't also written on the Wish card, *And be more like his father, Ernesto*. She tossed the phone on the unoccupied side of the bed, settled in with the pillows propped against the headboard and began reading the novel again, occasionally pausing to sip her warm cocoa.

A couple hours later, she was bleary eyed and couldn't read anymore. She focused on the clock, which read: 10:35. It felt like it was a lot later. Exhausted from an extremely busy week (she'd had no days off), she closed the book and placed it on the night stand. She clicked off the light and scrunched inside the covers. It wasn't long before she easily slipped into slumberland.

A short time later, she awakened and realized that she'd been dreaming, a rarity for Grace McBride. She looked at the clock and waited for her eyes to focus. It was 12:37 a.m. She had only been asleep two hours, and already dreams had invaded her sleep. Then she remembered: Christmas Eve, midnight mass, the Solteros. And she experienced a deep sense of regret for not having taken Ernesto's advice, summoned the gumption and joined the family for midnight mass. She could have slept in tomorrow morning and still arrived around noon at her brother's home in Marin County. *Oh, well, snooze you lose.* Graciella lay back down on her pillow and soon drifted off to sleep again.

What seemed like just a few minutes later, she awakened again, this time with a start. Something urged her to look over at the clock: 11:35. *What in the world? Did time somehow reverse itself?* She tried to shake the cobwebs loose, and checked the clock again to be sure. *Yes, just a few minutes past 11:30 p.m.* Apparently, she had been in a dream state when she'd first read the clock. That meant there was still time. But not much. She tossed back the covers, clicked on the light and bounded from bed.

Grace pulled open her closet, found the simplest two-piece outfit that was appropriate church attire and laid it on the bed. She went in to the bathroom to brush her teeth and comb her hair and slipped into the clothes. She threw on her winter coat, spun a muffler around her neck and found her keys. When she backed out of the garage, the Jaguar clock read: 11:47.

CHAPTER TWELVE

From her McKinley Park home, the drive downtown to the cathedral on a weekend day would normally take fifteen minutes. But as she navigated through the slushy snow flurries, and icy thoroughfares leading downtown, she found driving to be a nightmarish experience. Sacramento hadn't seen snow in nearly thirty years, and people in the west tend to forget to slow down in this type of inclement weather, she thought. But Grace heeded her own advice, for she knew that if she misjudged one sharp corner, she might possibly wrap her car around a light pole, and would never meet the Solteros in church.

The Cathedral of the Blessed Sacrament is located downtown at 11th Street on the K Street Mall. As K Street is closed from 14th Street all the way to Old Sacramento, one must know how to navigate around the one-way streets to reach the parking area near the cathedral. Grace did from years of driving to client meetings and events at the Sacramento Convention Center.

As she turned north on 10th, and made another right on J Street, suddenly her car lights illuminated a homeless man, pushing a shopping cart across the street. She slammed on the brakes. Although the vehicle didn't appear to hit him, when he disappeared from view, Grace panicked. She stopped the car, got out and saw that he had merely fallen in the slushy street.

"Are you alright?" she called out, trying to help the man to his feet.

"Just slipped, that's all. Not your fault, ma'am."

The man got up and slowly began pushing the cart again. Without turning around, he gestured with his left hand that she shouldn't worry. Seeing the dollar bill in her hand, Grace scurried across the street and tapped the man on the shoulder. "Here," she said, placing it in his palm. "Merry Christmas."

"Thank you, ma'am. Merry Christmas to y'all as well," he said, continuing to push the cart across the street.

Grace returned to her car and said a silent prayer that when she made the turn on 11th Street one of the four metered parking spaces in front of the cathedral might be vacant. But she knew better; this was Christmas Eve and midnight mass. It would take a miracle. And when she pulled up behind the four cars nestled in their parking spaces, she realized one would not avail itself to her tonight.

"Oh, great," she whispered. "What did I expect?"

The car crept closer as the headlights illuminated the empty steps of the cathedral, devoid of any activity. As she began to turnaround, suddenly two figures appeared from around the side of the church. As the people approached, Grace drew down her window halfway.

"'Scuse me! Would you happen to be parked over here?" She tried pointing behind her, but her arm was impeded by the window mount.

"Yes, we're leaving," said a woman, guiding an elderly man toward one of the four cars parked nearby. "My father got a little dizzy in church. So, I'm taking him home. Too much excitement," she smiled, as snow landed on her head scarf. "We'll be out shortly."

Grace backed her car around and aimed the headlights in their direction to aid the woman as she helped her father into the passenger seat. The woman tip-toed around the back of her vehicle and waved, signaling she was going as quickly as she could in the slush.

Saints be praised.

* * *

As Graciella got out of the car, her footsteps crunched on the thin layer of snow carpeting the concrete courtyard of the cathedral area. She tied a plain gray scarf over her head, allowing just a hint of her chestnut brown hair to peek through, and scooted in short, swift steps toward the church.

When she entered the foyer of the cathedral her footsteps echoed in the stillness. Peering through the leaded glass windows of the enormous wooden doors, she could see the church was completely filled. In fact, it was standing room only all the way past the baptismal font.

She opened the heavy door and stood for a time, looking at the backs of the heads in the rear pews. The mass had just begun, as the bishop and his procession were filing down the center aisle, approaching the altar. She did not spot any of the Solteros. Grace glanced around, checking to see whether they may be standing in the back, too, but no luck. Then she felt a sense of dread: what if the Solteros hadn't come after all? Perhaps Ernie was being overly optimistic that the family would join in the midnight celebration of Christ's birth. Or, more practically, as they had stepped outside onto the front porch, and found the streets littered with snow, may have decided to go back inside where it was warm. Maybe they just hadn't come after all.

But Graciella Ceccarelli had fought, clawed and schmoozed her way to success on one simple credo: never give up. So, she proceeded to make her way up the right aisle, peering into the pews for any sign of the Solteros, as the congregation joined in the entrance hymn "O Come All Ye Faithful" in one, loud stirring voice.

After creeping along some twenty rows in search of her friends, she decided this was a crazy idea, for if she continued on this mission, she might find herself at a cocktail reception some evening, trying to explain to a group of business associates what she had been doing trawling the aisles in the cathedral, alone at Midnight Mass. She returned to the back with her head down. She stood there with the other latecomers debating what to do next. Finally, she turned and exited the building.

Standing on the marble landing outside in the cold, night air she listened to the choir and orchestra inside producing the most beautifully muted, spiritual music. It tugged at her heart. She wished she could be sitting inside right this minute, singing loudly with friends or family at her side, instead of freezing in the snow alone on this winter's night.

To her left, through the tears, was the vacant, unfriendly K Street Mall, with nary a store nor coffee shop open at this hour. Everything in that direction appeared dark and foreboding, with the exception of the stately capitol dome lit up in the distance. She trudged down the stone steps slowly, despondently. And in her lonely despair for companionship, family and a dream of happiness, she began to cry.

Grace began walking back to her car. Suddenly she felt the need to wipe her sniffles, so she paused and reached into her coat pocket and drew out a handkerchief. She was grateful it had not been removed from the last time she wore this coat. And while standing in the snowdrifts of the cathedral courtyard, her peripheral vision discerned a light flickering off to her right between the old Presbytery building and the cathedral. Hanging above the north side entrance to the cathedral was a dim, yellow light that flickered on, then off, then on for a longer time, then off for several seconds, as if in its irregular pattern it was desperately trying to signal the disconsolate woman: *Try here*.

At first Grace was reluctant to go in that direction as the walkway was narrow, and poorly lit; a perfect place to be accosted or worse. But as she moved closer she saw footprints in the snow, leading in both directions, and realized that the couple who had recently exited the cathedral came from this side entrance. During that moment of contemplation, while staring at the doorway, debating her next move, the yellow light suddenly came on, stayed lit and flickered no more. She stood there, waiting for the lamp to turn dark again, but it remained on, glowing brightly. *If ever there was a sign*, she thought. Grace followed the footprints and the alluring warm glow of the courtyard lamp all the way inside the antechamber leading in to the cathedral.

Inside the dark, gray cloistered entry area she walked softly, peering timidly around the corner looking for her friends. The congregation was still standing, singing in unison. And as she drew near the doorway, she looked out at the beautifully carved swirling end caps that define each row. And the Old World-style craftsmanship reminded her of the Soltero workshop.

In this meditative moment, Grace was startled by a hand waving to draw her attention to the centermost pew framed in the archway. She looked up and saw the broad, friendly face of Jamas Soltero standing just a few feet away. His expression revealed concern, for Grace appeared as a cowering, faltering street waif come in from the cold. He waved her over. As she emerged from the darkness into the bright light of the cathedral, he stepped into the aisle, and made room for her in the pew, next to Donte Soltero.

Donte's comforting face and extended hand immediately warmed her heart. When she snuggled in next to him, he gave her a kiss on the cheek and helped remove her coat. In the pew in front of them, Ernesto, Alena and Anthony had all turned and greeted her with smiles. Ernie leaned over the bench and gave her a soft kiss on the other cheek. She scooted over to make room for Jamas, and heard Donte whisper in her ear.

"Glad you came."

She smiled. "Must be magic in the air."

He squeezed her hand and whispered, "But only for those who *believe*."

She smiled in return, her heart filled with love, her voice rejoicing in song.

As Graciella peered upward at the cathedral ceiling, she marveled at the exquisite beauty throughout this hallowed structure, but especially at the artwork depicting the heavens swirling inside the glorious dome that spanned overhead. Rimmed around the perimeter of the dome were cerulean skies, merging into cumulus clouds, brimming with brilliant sunlight, radiating around the circle in the center. Inside the circle, she saw a white dove flying across a divinely beautiful azure sky, offering a symbol of peace and love.

And this reminded her of the little Wish Holder sitting on her nightstand, which by some miraculous measure, had captured her heartfelt desire and revealed to her the inherent power of faith. All on a Christmas Eve.

-The End-

ABOUT THE AUTHOR

R. A. Cabral is a Sacramento native and a published author of fiction, non-fiction and feature articles.

The author's experience in a public relations agency, combined with his Portuguese heritage, provide a unique backdrop for this story about love, faith and magick in the 21st Century.

Coinciding with the reprinting of his novella, Mr. Cabral has adapted the novella into an audiobook dramatization. The author narrates and contributes the voices of the Soltero men. He is complemented by eight other actors who portray the book's other characters, mixed with music and sound effects to create a true dramatization of this work. The audiobook is available at Audible.com, Amazon.com or iTunes.

Mr. Cabral's other works include:

The Pitch: The Adventures of Luther Woundup and His Magical Orange Ball, a baseball fantasy, 2004, Amazon.com.

Against All Odds: How the River Cats Became Sacramento's Hometown Team, 2012, Amazon Digital Services, Inc.

Barnstormin' Across America: The Bustin' Babes and Larrupin' Lous, 2013, Amazon Digital Services, Inc.

Made in the USA
San Bernardino, CA
05 September 2016